"My head is full of nonsense…"

Amos narrowed his eyes. "You aren't nearly as out of touch with things as you would like your family to believe. I believe you're quite smart and intuitive."

Deborah's expression changed to a mix of shock and…pleasure? "You think I'm smart?"

"I told you that you need to tell me where you're going."

She gave him a tight smile. "You weren't here." She turned toward the buggy. "You want me to help you with finishing up?"

He should press the issue, but he didn't want to argue with her, didn't want to scare her away. "I would like that. Next time, tell someone where you're going. I know you don't understand or believe it, but I do feel responsible for everyone."

"But you're not. I can take care of myself."

But he wanted to look after her. "Sometimes your family may not notice you, but I do."

And she rewarded him with a sweet smile that made his brain a little fuzzy.

Mary Davis is an award-winning author of more than a dozen novels. She is a member of American Christian Fiction Writers and is active in two critique groups. Mary lives in the Colorado Rocky Mountains with her husband of thirty years and three cats. She has three adult children and one grandchild. Her hobbies are quilting, porcelain doll making, sewing, crafts, crocheting and knitting. Please visit her website, marydavisbooks.com.

Books by Mary Davis

Love Inspired

Prodigal Daughters

Courting Her Amish Heart
Courting Her Secret Heart

Love Inspired Heartsong Presents

Her Honorable Enemy
Romancing the Schoolteacher
Winning Olivia's Heart

Visit the Author Profile page at Harlequin.com for more titles.

Courting Her
Secret Heart

Mary Davis

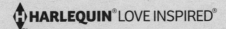

Recycling programs
for this product may
not exist in your area.

LOVE INSPIRED BOOKS

ISBN-13: 978-1-335-50970-3

Courting Her Secret Heart

www.Harlequin.com

Printed in U.S.A.

No man can serve two masters: for either he will hate the one, and love the other; or else he will hold to the one, and despise the other. Ye cannot serve God and mammon.

—*Matthew* 6:24

German Proverb: *Wer zwei Hasen auf einmal jagt bekommt keinen.*

"He who chases two rabbits at once will catch none."

Dedicated to my awesome sister Deborah Spencer.

A special thanks to Melissa Endlich
and the editorial team at Love Inspired and to
Sarah Joy Freese and WordServe Literary Agency.
I'm so thankful to work with you!

Chapter One

Elkhart County, Indiana

Deborah Miller ran to the clump of bare sycamore trees at the far edge of the pond on her family's property. Fortunately, the latest round of snow had melted and the ground had dried, so she wouldn't be leaving tracks.

Several ducks squawked their disapproval of her presence. With indignation, they waddled and flapped onto the frozen water.

Deborah cringed. "Sorry to disturb you. I'll bring you some bread crusts tomorrow."

The largest tree in the grove had a tangle of many trunks from its base, creating an empty space in the center. She scurried over and dropped her green, tan and white camouflage backpack into the hollow. A sprinkle of dried leaves on top, and no one would ever find it. Truth be told, she could leave her pack out in the open and no one would likely notice it. It would blend in with the tree's patchwork bark.

She took off for the house, running between the stubbly winter cornfield rows. She was going to be late.

She'd lost track of time, which was her usual excuse, but this time it was true. She could be gone all day and no one in her family ever noticed her absence. Or if they did, they never mentioned it. Apparently, keeping track of so many girls was too much trouble to bother with. Seven. And she was right smack-dab in the middle. Not the oldest. Not the youngest. Not anything.

Of late, everyone was fussing over Hannah and Lydia, who were both planning to marry this fall. Although no one was supposed to know, since neither wedding would be officially announced until late summer or early fall, but a lot of celery would be planted in the garden this spring. After all, they couldn't have Amish weddings without celery.

It had been a *gut* photo shoot today. The sun was shining, and though cold out, it had been a perfect day. Even if by some strange chance her absence had been noticed and she got scolded for being gone, it wouldn't dampen her mood. Nothing could spoil today.

Deborah pulled her coat tighter around herself as she slowed down and entered the yard, finding it oddly quiet. She needed to look as though she hadn't been in a hurry and just lost track of time, as usual.

Chickens pecked at the ground, but no people could be seen. Where was everyone? Were *all* her sisters in the house with *Mutter*? That was peculiar. One or two were often outside at this time of day. Unusual to have caught them all in the kitchen.

An Amish man came out of the barn, carrying two empty buckets.

Who was he? She'd never seen him before. Though dressed Amish, she had to wonder if he belonged to their community. His light brown hair peeked out from under his black felt hat. The brim shaded his face. Just the type of rugged Amish man that Hudson, her photographer, had repeatedly asked her to find for photo shoots. What was this stranger doing on their farm?

She approached him. "Who are you?" Her words puffed out on little white clouds.

"I'm Amos Burkholder. Who are you?" He smiled.

A warm, inviting, disarming smile. The kind that could make her forget her purpose. A smile she wouldn't mind retreating into. She mentally shook herself free of his spell. "I'm Deborah Miller. I live here. What are you doing on our farm? And where's my family?"

"Deborah? I was told the whole family went to the hospital. What are *you* doing here?"

"Hospital? Why?" Her family went to the hospital and hadn't noticed her absence? It figured.

"Bartholomew Miller had an accident. An ambulance came. Bishop Bontrager asked me to take care of things here until you all returned and your *vater* was able to work again."

"My *vater*? Accident? What happened? Is he all right?"

"I don't know the details. But if the bishop thinks your *vater* will be well enough to work his farm again, then I think he will be all right eventually. Would you like me to drive you into Goshen to the hospital?"

Deborah shook her head. "If I hitch up the smaller buggy, I can drive myself."

"I'll hitch it."

"Danki." Deborah ran into the house to grab her bag of sewing. In case she had a while to wait at the hospital, she wanted to have something to keep herself distracted from too much worry. When she came back out, Amos wasn't much further along in getting the buggy ready.

Impatient, Deborah stalked over to the horse standing in the yard and took hold of the harness on the other side from Amos.

He stopped his progress. "I'm capable of doing this myself."

Deborah hooked the belly strap. "I know." What Amish person didn't know how to hitch up a horse to a buggy by themselves by age ten or twelve? "If I help, it'll go faster."

After a deep breath, he got back to the work at hand. Once the buggy was hitched and ready to go, he climbed in the side opposite her and took charge of the reins.

She put her hands on her hips. "What are you doing?"

"Taking you into town."

"I told you that I can drive a buggy myself."

"I know and have no doubt you're capable, but you're flustered over the news of your *vater*, and it would be best if you don't drive in your present state."

"Present state? What's that supposed to mean?"

He tilted his head. "Are you getting in? Or would you rather walk to town?"

With a huff, she climbed aboard and plopped down on the seat. "You are insufferable."

He handed her a quilt for her lap, then gently snapped the reins and clucked the horse into motion. "If by *insufferable* you mean *helpful*, then *danki*."

Why was she being so ill-tempered? This wasn't like her. Maybe it was the news of her *vater* being injured. Or maybe it was her guilt of being away from the house when it happened. Or maybe it was because she knew she had been doing something her *vater*, her family and the community would frown upon. Or maybe it was all three. Whatever the reason, Amos didn't deserve her poor attitude when he was being so helpful and kind. "I'm sorry for being difficult. I'm worried about my *vater*."

"That's understandable."

She blew into her hands to warm them, then slipped on her knitted mittens. "I haven't seen you before. Do you belong to a neighboring community district?"

"*Ne*. We live on the other side of the district. We moved here a year ago from Pennsylvania. We're at church every other Sunday. You've even been to church at our farm. We obviously haven't made a memorable impression on you. Or at least I haven't."

How could she not remember him? "Tell me a little about your family to remind me."

"I am the youngest of five boys. The two oldest stayed in Pennsylvania and split the farm we had there."

"I think I know who you are, or at least your family. I'm the middle of seven girls."

"I know. I've seen you in church along with all your sisters."

He'd noticed her?

"Tell me something, is Miriam spoken for or being courted by anyone?"

Evidently, he had his eye on her sister, who was a little over a year older than herself. That meant, it hadn't been Deborah he'd noticed at church, but her sister. Disappointing. Someone else who overlooked her. "Timothy Zook seems interested in her."

"Is she interested in him?"

"Some days *ja*, and others *ne*. Miriam likes a lot of boys. She can't seem to decide which one she likes most. She's so afraid of choosing the wrong man to marry, we fear she'll never marry at all." Deborah pulled a face. "I probably shouldn't have told you all that. Please don't hold it against her. She's a very wonderful sister."

His chuckle held no humor.

Was it truly Miriam she didn't want him to think of poorly, or herself because of her derogatory words? Why should she care what this man thought of her? But she did. "Can you hurry? I need to know how my *vater* is."

"I'm going as fast as the *Ordnung* allows."

"But this is kind of an emergency. You would be allowed to go faster."

He thinned his lips. "This isn't an emergency. Your *vater's* being well looked after. Whether it takes us five minutes or five hours to get there will have no bearing on your *vater's* condition."

He was right, of course, but she had already missed so much. She very much wished they were going by car. "When was my *vater* hurt?"

"First thing this morning."

So long ago? He must have gotten hurt soon after she had slipped away. Now she really did feel guilty.

Like Amos said, if she got to the hospital with everyone else or in the next hour, she wouldn't have been able to make a difference. But at least she could have been with her family. And know what was going on.

She settled her nerves for the plodding, boring journey. "Do you miss Pennsylvania?"

"Ne."

That was a sharp reply.

"But you grew up there. Your friends are there. The rest of your family is there. Don't you miss any of them?"

"Ne."

Again, his single word sounded harsh.

"There's nothing for me back there. This move was supposed to be *gut*."

But she sensed it wasn't. She wanted to press him, to understand why he seemed to harbor bitterness toward the place where he'd grown up, but doubted he would tell her anything. After all, they were basically strangers.

Eventually, Amos pulled in next to several other buggies outside the hospital.

She jumped out. "You don't have to stay. I'll get a ride back with my family. *Danki.*" She trotted inside. She inquired at the information desk and soon found her family, with all her sisters, as well as several other community members. Her *vater* sat in a wheelchair, waiting to be discharged.

His left arm rested in a sling, and his left leg was in a cast and propped on a pillow on one of the wheelchair's leg supports. He'd chosen neon green. Would the church leaders approve of the color? Probably not, but they wouldn't be able to do anything about it until he had the cast changed in a few weeks.

Thirteen-year-old Naomi made a face at her.

Deborah ignored her younger sister, who liked to stir up trouble, and hurried over to him. "*Vater*, are you all right?"

Vater gave her a lopsided smile. "I'm feeling great. They gave me something for the pain. But I don't have any pain."

"There you are, Deborah." Her *mutter* frowned. "I was wondering where you'd gotten off to. Did you go to the vending machines without telling me?"

Vending machines? Hadn't her *mutter* noticed that Deborah had only just now arrived? That she'd been absent all day? Was she truly invisible to her family? Did any of them even care? No wonder she could be gone for hours and hours without repercussions. No one ever realized her absence.

Amos joined them then. "How are you doing, Mr. Miller?"

Vater waved his hands aimlessly through the air. "It's Bartholomew. I don't have any pain."

Deborah turned to Amos. "I thought you left."

"If you would have waited, I would have walked in with you." He turned to *Mutter*. "I brought Deborah."

Mutter gave Deborah a double take. "You weren't here? Then where were you?"

Oh, dear. "I went for a walk, and before I knew it, I had gone farther than I realized, and it took me a while to get back home."

"Oh." *Mutter* turned back to the nurse behind *Vater's* wheelchair. "Are we leaving now? I want to leave now. I have supper to start."

"We need to wait for the doctor to sign the release papers."

How had any of them survived infancy and childhood with *Mutter* always forgetting things? Well, mostly forgetting Deborah. She didn't have trouble with the rest of her daughters. Just her middlemost one.

The familiar pang of being left out twisted around her heart. One of these days, she might decide not to return. Would her *mutter* even notice? Probably not.

Well, it *had been* a perfect day until she'd come home and found out her world had been turned upside down.

Amos's inviting brown gaze settled on her. She wished now the buggy ride had taken longer. His look of sympathy warmed her heart. Well, at least *he* acknowledged her presence.

Amos studied Miriam, who smiled at everyone in the hospital waiting room. Did she truly like a lot of young men? Or was she just really nice? He'd been fooled by girls before. More than once. His gaze shifted back to Deborah. She stood on the edge of the crowd, with them but not really a part of them. How could no one have noticed she hadn't been with the family when they left for the hospital? Or at least once they arrived. He admired how she seemed to take that in stride. The hospital lights didn't spark the red hints in her hair the way the sun had.

Deborah turned to him, and he smiled at her without thinking. Her green eyes seemed as though she could see his broken heart. There was something more to her than met the eye. Something he couldn't quite figure out. Like she had some sort of secret. Probably just his own guilty conscience. He didn't want to look away, but he did.

From down the hall, a man stared at him. It was his cousin Jacob. His shunned cousin Jacob, who'd left the Amish church and community. He glanced back at the crowd of his fellow Amish waiting for Bartholomew to be released.

He moved around the crowd to Bishop Bontrager. "I have something I need to take care of. Will you let the Millers know that I'll meet them back at their farm?"

The bishop nodded. "*Ja. Danki* for agreeing to lend them a hand. Bartholomew is going to be laid up for some time. Will your *vater* be able to spare you to stay on at the Millers'?"

"*Ja.* I'm sure he can." His *vater* had already declared the farm not big enough for Amos. He glanced in the direction where Jacob had been. "I won't be far behind everyone." As he hurried down the hall, he threw a glance back over his shoulder at Deborah and almost went back to her, but didn't. When he turned the corner, he came upon his cousin, who was leaning against the wall. Jacob looked strange but *gut* in his *English* clothes, jeans and a hooded sweatshirt. They suited his cousin. "What are you doing here?"

"I saw you drive up with one of the Miller girls. Quite a collection of Amish you're with. None of them *your* family, though. *And* the bishop."

"Bartholomew Miller broke his leg." Amos glanced back to make sure no one had followed him. "The bishop asked me to help out at their farm while they took him to the hospital."

Jacob nodded. "You seemed pretty content with all of them. Are you still interested in leaving?"

Amos's insides knotted. This would be a life-changing decision, but he didn't see the use of the Amish life anymore. His *vater* didn't have land enough for all his sons, and the Amish girls here seemed no different from the flighty ones back in Pennsylvania. Except Deborah. She seemed different. But that was what he'd thought about Esther. And Bethany. "*Ja*, of course I am."

"It might take a few weeks to get everything set up. I'll be in touch with more information."

"I'll wait to hear from you." Once away from the community and no longer having to keep this a secret, he'd feel better about his decision. "I should go before they get suspicious." Amos could be shunned just for talking to an ex-Amish member. But once he left, he would be shunned and turned over to the devil and ex-communicated from the church, as well.

"See you soon." Jacob walked off in the opposite direction of the waiting room.

Amos peeked around the corner. None of his Amish brethren remained, only a handful of *Englishers*. He straightened before heading down the hall and out to the buggy parking area.

The only buggy that remained was the one he'd driven into town. Deborah sat on the buggy seat, rubbing her mitten-clad hands briskly together. She turned in his direction, and his heart sped up.

He stopped beside the vehicle. Though she wore a *kapp*, the sun once again ignited the hints of red in her hair around her face. "What are you still doing here? Why didn't you go with the others?"

The quilt lay across her lap. "All the other buggies were full."

That was a little sad. She'd been left behind. Now he felt bad for making her wait.

She picked up the reins and tilted her head. "Are you getting in? Or would you rather walk?"

Throwing his words back at him? Little scamp. But she'd lightened his mood. He climbed in and extended his hands for the reins.

She moved them from his reach and snapped the horse into motion.

He couldn't believe she'd just done that. It was audacious. "I should drive."

"Why?"

"Because I'm the man and you're a woman."

She set her jaw and kept control of the reins. "I'm quite capable, *danki*."

She certainly seemed so, as well as a little bit feisty. He wanted to drive, but unless he wrestled the reins away from her, it didn't seem likely. "Did I do something to upset you?"

"Ne." Her answer was short and clipped.

"It certainly seems like I did. No one else around for you to be angry at."

She tossed the reins into his lap. "Take them if you want to drive so badly."

Now he had vexed her. He didn't want the reins this way and was tempted to leave them where they were, but that wouldn't do for the horse to have no guidance. With the reins in hand, he pulled to the side of the street in front of an antique store and stopped. "If I haven't upset you, then what has?"

She took a slow breath, and for a moment, he doubted she would answer him, but then she let out a huff of white air. "It doesn't matter."

"*Ja*, it does. Tell me." Why did it bother him so much that she was upset? He should just let it go and get back to her family's farm.

"My family went off to the hospital and didn't notice I wasn't with them."

That could be quite upsetting, but he'd thought that hadn't bothered her. He'd been wrong. "They were probably all worried about your *vater*. Focused on getting him the care he needed."

She sat quietly for a moment, and he could almost feel her mood shift. "You're right. I was being selfish. Only thinking of myself. I have a habit of doing that. *Danki*."

He smiled. *"Bitte."* He liked that he could help her and appreciated her honesty. Something he'd found lacking in others.

She waved her mittened hand in the air. "Shall we go?"

He lifted the reins but then paused and handed them over to her. "You can drive."

The smile she gifted him with and the spark in her green eyes as she took the reins warmed him all over.

Chapter Two

Amos sat forward on the buggy seat as the Miller farm came into view. What would people think of him not driving? He was the man, after all. He *should* be driving. Instinct told him to take the reins, but something held him back. He gritted his teeth, hoping no one would be out in the yard.

Deborah pulled on one rein and slackened the other to turn into the driveway.

Though several buggies, the chickens and two cats were scattered about the yard, fortunately no people were in sight.

She stopped the buggy in front of the house. "Do you mind putting this away by yourself? I want to see how my *vater's* doing."

He gladly took the offered reins. "I'd be happy to." He breathed easier having the strips of leather in his hands. How foolish of him, but he couldn't help feeling that way. "Tell your *vater* not to worry about the animals. I'll take care of everything."

"*Danki.* But I think he probably still has enough pain medication in him to not worry about much of anything right now." She jogged up the porch steps and into the house.

He stared at the door for a moment, feeling a sense of loss. But that couldn't be. He hadn't lost anything. At least not anything new. With a shake of his head, he drove the buggy to the barn. After unhitching the horse, he put the animal in a stall, then parked the buggy in its space inside the barn. Being an open buggy, it needed to be protected from the elements. With the harness put away, he brushed down the horse and fed him.

His encounter with his cousin Jacob played in his head. He needed to get off his *vater's* farm and experience the outside world more than he had on *Rumspringa*, with a different purpose this time. If he wasn't going to have land to farm and would have to work in the *Englisher* world anyway, he might as well live there, too, and be a part of it.

Amos would have left the first time when Jacob suggested it if there had been some place for him to go, but today was a different matter. The image of Deborah standing on the edge of her family at the hospital tugged at his heart. She needed him. This family needed him. Bartholomew needed him. And he needed them so he wouldn't have to be on his family's farm until he left for *gut*. This would make the wait more bearable.

He heard the humming of a female enter the barn. Deborah? He peeked out of the stall he was in as someone disappeared into the stall with the milking cow, but he couldn't tell who. He brushed down the front of his coat and trousers to remove hay particles, then stepped into the stall doorway.

Miriam glanced up at him with a smile from where she sat on a three-legged stool. "*Hallo*, Amos Burkholder."

His smile sagged a bit. "*Hallo*." This was *gut* that it

wasn't Deborah. He shouldn't be thinking of her. "Your job to milk the cow?"

She leaned her head against the animal's side and began the task with a *swish-swish-swish. "Ja."*

"Do you and your sisters trade off with this duty?"

"*Ne*, I like milking. There is something soothing about it. It's just me and Sybil."

"I'm sorry. Would you like me to go away?"

"Ne."

He wasn't sure if he was disappointed or not at having to stay. "Tell me about your sisters."

"What do you want to know?"

"I don't know. I figure if I'm going to be working on your farm, I should know a little about everyone."

She nodded. "Hannah and Lydia are twins—identical. Hannah is the ultraresponsible one. Lydia is the peacemaker. They are both being courted and will likely get married this fall. Then comes me. A lot of people say I'm the positive one. I do try to see the *gut* in situations."

That was not how Deborah had described her. What was it she had said? That Miriam liked a lot of boys. Likely, there wasn't one young man in particular who had caught her attention yet.

"Then Deborah. After her comes Joanna. She's the *gut* one. Not that the rest of us aren't *gut*, but she was an easy baby and has always been easy to please. She's also quite shy. Naomi's thirteen and can be moody. She likes to be the center of attention. And lastly is carefree baby Sarah at eight. She is easily everyone's favorite, and the sweetest of us all."

Everyone got a description except Deborah. "What about Deborah?"

"What about her?"

"You gave everyone a little description except her."

"Did I? Hmm. Deborah is...irres—rarely here."

Was she about to say *irresponsible*? True, Deborah hadn't been around when her *vater* had been hurt, but that didn't necessarily make her irresponsible.

When Miriam finished milking, Amos hoisted the full bucket and carried it to the house.

Miriam opened the door to the kitchen and allowed him to enter first. The kitchen bustled with female activity. He was used to just his *mutter* in the kitchen, alone, doing all the work by herself.

Deborah looked up from her task of churning butter with the youngest girl and smiled at him.

He responded in kind.

Her gaze flickered away from him to where Miriam appeared, and Deborah's smile faltered, then she pushed her mouth up in a less genuine smile, but one of encouragement.

He wished he could bring back that first smile. What had caused the change? More important, how could he bring back the first smile?

"Right this way, Amos." Miriam motioned with her hand for him to follow her. "That goes in the back fridge until morning."

Amos aimed his apologetic shrug toward Deborah as he obediently complied. When he returned, Deborah's *mutter* stood in his path.

Teresa Miller put her hands on her hips and gave him an impish smile. "We do so love company, but you can't walk through my kitchen without introducing yourself."

"I'm Amos Burkholder."

"Which one of my daughters are you courting?"

"Um, none. I'm here to help out on the farm while Bartholomew is healing."

Shock and concern wiped away the older woman's smile in an instant. "What? What's wro—"

One of the older girls hooked her arm around her *mutter's* shoulders and escorted her out of the kitchen. "Let's go see how *Vater* is doing."

Another of the older sisters stood in front of him. "Supper will be ready in a little bit. We'll call you when it's ready."

This must be Lydia, the peacemaker. The one who left with their *mutter* must have been Hannah, the ultra-responsible one. Or it could be vice versa. He wasn't sure. He nodded and went back outside to finish up some chores.

Soon, another one of the sisters came out to retrieve him. "Supper's ready." She kept her head down.

"*Danki.* I'll head in with you." He walked to her side. "I didn't mean to upset your *mutter* earlier."

Her head remained down and her voice soft. "You didn't. She was just worried about *Vater.*"

It had seemed like more than worry. But then, what did he know?

This shy girl must be Joanna. It would probably be best if he didn't stress her by trying to hold a meaning-less conversation just to quiet the silence.

Inside, he washed up and waited to be told where he should sit at the table.

Bartholomew sat alone at the far end of the table, his broken leg propped up on a chair. The women still scurried to and fro.

The youngest, who looked to be more like five than eight, crashed into him and wrapped her chubby arms around his waist. "Broffer Amos."

He wasn't sure what to make of this little one. "*Hallo*, Sarah."

She giggled.

One of the twins, he guessed Lydia, hurried over and disentangled the young one from him. "I'm sorry about that. She likes to greet people with a hug."

"That's all right." He gazed down into the upturned face of Sarah. Her slanted eyes and flat nose told him all he needed to know. Down syndrome. "I'm very pleased to meet you."

Lydia smiled at him but spoke to Sarah. "Go sit down. It's time to eat."

Sarah grabbed his hand. "Sit by me."

He looked to Lydia, who gave him a nod. He sat, and quickly the others did so, as well. Bartholomew blessed the food, and everyone served themselves except Sarah. Hannah, who sat on her other side, dished up for her.

Bartholomew grimaced in pain. His medication had probably worn off. "Amos, I certainly do appreciate you coming to help out in my hour of need."

"I'm glad to be here."

Teresa tilted her head. "Hour? It'll be a mite more than that." Her anxiety from earlier had been erased.

The girl directly across from Amos crinkled her nose. "I bet you don't even know who all of us are."

Center of attention. "You're Naomi."

He went around the table and named each of the family members.

Naomi narrowed her eyes. She obviously didn't think he could do it.

He wasn't so sure himself but had guessed right. Miriam's descriptions had helped. When he'd named Deborah and she smiled at him, something inside did a little flip. That was the smile he'd been looking for. He wanted to stop and stare at her but knew he shouldn't.

He cleared his throat to regain his train of thought

and shifted his attention to Bartholomew. "I could, of course, travel home each night and return in the morning, but I would be able to get more work accomplished if I stayed on here."

Bartholomew swallowed his mouthful of food. "What did you have in mind?"

"I thought I could sleep in the barn."

Teresa spoke up. "I won't hear of that. The barn is no place for a person in winter."

Bartholomew gazed gently at his *frau*. "What would you suggest, *Mutter*?"

"Joanna and Naomi can move in with Miriam and…" She waved her hand in Deborah's direction. "And her sister."

A sadness flickered across Deborah's face, and Amos's heart ached for her. He knew what it was like to be hurt by family.

Naomi leaned forward. "I don't want to move rooms and be crowded in."

"Hush," Bartholomew scolded his daughter, and she huffed and folded her arms. Then he turned back to his *frau*. "You would have a young man who isn't a family member under the same roof as our daughters?"

Teresa's gaze flittered around the table, and the inappropriateness of the situation registered on her face. "Oh. I…"

Amos didn't want to cause a fuss. "I don't want to displace anyone. The barn will be fine. There's an old woodstove still connected in the tack room. I can move a few things around and set up a cot." It was preferable to home.

With supper concluded and the arrangements settled, Amos headed out to fix up his new but temporary living quarters.

He located some firewood and lit the stove. Then he made a clearing in the center of the room and set up the cot that was used when an animal was sick and someone needed to stay in the barn to keep a watchful eye out.

A gray tabby rubbed against his leg. He crouched and petted him. "What's your name, hmm?"

The cat sauntered over to the stove, sniffed it and lay down in front of it.

"Don't get too comfortable. You can't stay in here at night with the door closed. You can warm yourself until I find some blankets."

When he exited the tack room, Deborah stood outside his door with an armful of quilts. She smiled. "We thought you might need these." She handed him the pile. "There's a pillow, as well."

"*Danki.* These'll be better than the horse blankets I was planning to rustle up."

"*Bitte.*" Her gaze lingered on him a long moment before she turned to leave.

He wanted to say something to make her stay. But what use would there be in that? Instead, he watched her walk out.

The following morning, Deborah stole glances at Amos throughout breakfast. Several times, she caught him looking back at her.

Vater hadn't come to the table for breakfast. Fortunately, his and *Mutter's* bedroom was on the main floor, so he wouldn't have to go up and down the stairs with a broken leg and injured arm. Though *Mutter* had scurried around the kitchen earlier, she had gone in to sit with *Vater.* Since *Vater's* accident, less than a day ago, *Mutter* had acted stranger than usual. One moment she sat calmly, and the next she scampered about like a nervous squirrel looking for lost acorns.

Amos drained the last of his coffee. "*Danki* for breakfast. I should get to work."

"Would you like another cup?" For some reason, she didn't want him to leave yet. It was nice having another man around the farm. Or was it that it was just different for all the girls? Or was it having a kind, handsome, eligible man around?

His mouth curved up into a smile that tickled her insides. "*Danki.* Maybe later." He gazed at her for a moment before trudging outside.

After he left, she stared at the door for a bit longer than she should before she turned to her sisters. "What do you need me to do?"

Lydia had taken charge of the kitchen cleanup. "I think we have everything covered."

Her sisters bustled around, busy at work. Even Naomi helped, and Sarah had her little job of sorting the silverware. The only other one not there, besides their parents, was Hannah.

Deborah headed for her parents' room and peeked in around the door frame. "Is there anything I can do? Anything you need?"

Mutter held a plate while *Vater* ate with his *gut* arm.

Hannah gingerly tucked a pillow under *Vater's* broken leg. "We're *gut*. See if the others need help in the kitchen."

Deborah gave a weak smile. She'd already done that. "*Vater*, I'm praying you heal quickly."

"*Danki.*"

She left. With nothing to do inside, she headed outside and found Amos in the barn.

He stood below the hayloft, staring up at the underside of the floor above.

"What are you doing?"

He turned to her, and his mouth pulled up at the corners. "Trying to decide the best way to fix this."

She liked his smile. A lot. She stood next to him and looked to where he pointed. A hole roughly the size of a laundry basket had opened up through several of the boards, and hay hung down in the opening. "What happened?"

Shifting, he stared at her. "You really don't know?"

"Know what?"

"Your *vater* fell through there and landed here on the floor. Fortunately, there weren't any tools, boxes or barrels for him to get further injured on."

She pictured her *vater* falling and gasped. She hadn't thought to ask just how he'd gotten hurt. All she knew was that he had fallen.

"The boards look pretty rotted. They should have been replaced long before now."

"Why hadn't he done that?"

"He was probably too busy with running the rest of the farm on his own to notice. I'll check all the boards and build a new loft floor if need be. I figure I can do some of the regular maintenance he couldn't get to and repair what needs repairing until I… Until it's time to plow and plant."

"Do you think he's going to be in a cast that long?"

"Hard to say. Some people's bones heal faster than others'. But even if he's out of the cast, his leg will be weak. He'll need time to regain his strength."

"What can I do to help?"

He chuffed out a chuckle. "What? I'm sure there's plenty to be done in the house."

"Hannah and Lydia are taking care of *Vater* while overseeing the breakfast cleanup as well as the early prep for lunch. Everyone's busy with their regular duties, leaving nothing for me except free time." She didn't even have a modeling job today. That would have been nice to get her mind off *Vater* being hurt.

"This isn't woman's work."

"If you haven't noticed, my *vater* has seven girls. We've all done a bit of carpentry, livestock tending and even some plowing. So let me help."

"*Danki* for the offer, but I can manage."

If she was a man, he'd accept her help. "Well, I have nothing else to do, so I'm not leaving." She backed up to a covered feed barrel, pushed herself up and sat. "If you won't let me help with the labor, I'll supervise from here." The truth was, she just wanted to be out here with him.

He stared at her hard for a long moment. "*You* are going to tell *me* how to fix this?"

"It's either that or put me to work." The work would go faster if he allowed her to help. Would he be too stubborn and insist on doing it alone? If so, he deserved to have a more difficult time than need be, *and* he deserved to have her comment on every little thing he did.

"Fine. But you have to do as I say. I don't want you getting hurt, as well."

She hopped off the barrel and saluted him.

He shook his head at her playful gesture. "First we need to determine how sturdy the rest of this floor is." He handed her a shovel, and he grabbed a pitchfork for himself. "Tap the underside of the boards with the end of the handle." He demonstrated with his implement.

Deborah poked at a board to show him that not only did she understand his elementary instructions, but that she could also follow his directions as ordered. Then she smiled.

He worked his mouth back and forth, presumably to keep from smiling himself. His effort created a cute expression.

She studied her shovel from tip to end. She didn't like the idea of lifting the heavy metal blade up and down. The repetitive movement would give her sore muscles, for sure. After looking around, she leaned the shovel against the wall and grabbed a push broom. Putting her foot on the head, she twisted the handle several times, freeing it. This was lighter. Much better for repetitive motions. She twirled it around once and went to work tapping and poking. "Tell me about your family."

Amos shrugged. "Like what?"

"Parents. Siblings."

"I have two parents and four brothers."

Not very forthcoming with information. She was going to have to work harder at learning anything about him. She would start with something easy and hope he got the hint and freely offered up more details. "What are your parents' names?"

"Joseph and Karen."

At least half the boards she poked at were usable for the time being, although they would need to be replaced soon. The other half of them were splintery and soft. "What about your brothers?"

"James, Boaz, Daniel and Titus."

She felt like growling and poking *him* with a stick. Couldn't he give her more information? Did he not want to talk to her? Well, she wasn't about to work in silence. Her sisters chatted all the time while doing chores. "Where do you fit into all of them?"

"Youngest."

Really? Nothing more than that? She did growl now, softly to herself, and jabbed her stick at the next board. It poked through, splintering the wood in half. Hay showered down on her from between the dangling halves.

Amos rushed over and pulled her out of the way as one of the jagged pieces broke free and shot straight down to where she'd been standing. She could have been seriously injured.

Caught off guard by his action, she lost her balance and grasped at his sleeve. Her body twisted, and gravity did the rest of the work, landing her in a pile of straw.

Between her yanking on his sleeve and his trying to catch her, he lost his footing as well and landed in the straw beside her with one arm stretched across to the other side of her. His eyes went wide. "Are you all right? Did you get hurt?"

He looked so adorable in his worried state that a giggle escaped her lips before she could stop it.

His mouth pulled up at the corners. "I guess that means you're not hurt."

She nodded and wrestled her chortling under control.

He plucked hay off her cheek and forehead. "You're covered."

She imagined she was but didn't help him, liking his ministrations.

His hand stilled, and he stared down at her for a long moment.

What was he thinking?

Clearing his throat, he pushed himself up to his feet, then offered her assistance. His hand was large and strong. And warm.

As soon as she was on her feet, he released her quickly as though embarrassed, and stared up at the ceiling. "Too many of the boards are rotted beyond repair, and the ones that are serviceable won't be for long. It would be best to replace the whole floor. I'll take the wagon into town and order the necessary lumber."

Now he was chatty? Or had their little moment made him uncomfortable? She missed the moment of closeness they'd just shared. Would they have another one in the future? She hoped so.

Chapter Three

The next morning, Amos was sent into town by the oldest twin, Hannah, to pick up some medicine for Bartholomew Miller. Though identical in most respects, he noted that Hannah had a worry crease between her eyebrows, which helped him to differentiate the two sisters.

He now drove back along the paved road. Floyd plodded along. The rhythm of his clip-clopping hoofbeats lulled Amos's thoughts—thoughts that drifted to his cousin. Jacob was *gut* to help Amos. Amos wouldn't know what to do on the outside. Having his cousin's guidance made him feel less anxious about the whole endeavor. Jacob knew all about Amos's hurts back in Pennsylvania. How Esther had let him court her and led him to believe she cared for him, only to turn down his offer of marriage. Then when he'd arrived in Indiana, the situation was nearly repeated with Bethany.

Then his thoughts turned to the Millers' farm. The work there was *gut*. Gave him purpose. And being around all those women would give him insight into the female mind. Maybe then he could figure out what he'd done wrong in the past.

Up ahead, an Amish woman meandered in the middle of the two-lane country road.

What was she doing?

A car came down the road, honked and swerved around her.

She sidestepped but didn't move to the side of the road.

He snapped the reins to hurry the horse. When he pulled up beside her, he said, "Ma'am?"

She faced him but didn't really look at him.

"Teresa? Teresa Miller?" He hauled back on the reins.

"Ja." She raised her hand to shade her eyes from the morning winter sun.

"What are you doing out here?"

"I was going somewhere." She chuckled. "But I seem to have forgotten where."

That didn't explain why she was in the middle of the road. He jumped down. "Come. I'll drive you home."

"That would be nice. *Danki.*" She climbed into the buggy and waited.

How odd. But other than her being in the middle of the road, he couldn't put his finger on what exactly was off about this encounter. He got in and took her home.

When he drove into the yard and up to the house, the twins rushed outside without coats on. Hannah opened the buggy door and took Teresa's hand. *"Mutter*, where have you been? We've been looking for you." A forced cheeriness laced her words.

"I went for a nice little walk." She patted Amos's arm. "But I was safe."

Hannah helped her *mutter* out and exchanged glances with Lydia. Hannah's gaze flickered to him. *"Danki."*

"Bitte." Amos held out the paper sack with the prescription. "Here's your *vater's* medication."

Lydia took it. *"Danki."* The women rushed into the house, leaving Amos to wonder.

Women. They behaved strangely. How was a man to figure them out? Maybe it was impossible, and he should give up on them altogether.

A while after Miriam had completed the late-afternoon milking, Amos headed to the house for supper. Though he'd been mulling over this morning's incident with Teresa all day and wanted to ask about it, he decided not to embarrass her by mentioning anything.

He stepped through the kitchen door into barely ordered chaos. One girl went this way while another went that way and two others looked to be on a collision course, but both swerved in the appropriate directions and barely missed running into each other. The women seemed to almost read each others' minds with each one going in a different direction. How did they ever get anything accomplished? But somehow they managed to pull supper together.

Maybe there was some order to their mayhem he couldn't detect. That men in general couldn't. He would like to figure it out but sensed he could spend a lifetime and never understand women. He should give up even trying anymore.

Teresa Miller smiled and came over to him. "My brother stopped by and brought some of your things. They are in a suitcase by the front door."

"Your brother?"

"Ja. David. He wore that blue shirt I made him for his birthday."

Hannah gave a nervous-sounding giggle, and the crease between her eyebrows deepened. "She meant *your* brother."

He didn't have a brother named David. Maybe she meant Daniel.

"*Ne*. I didn't—"

Lydia put her arm around Teresa, effectively distracting her. "*Mutter*, did you get the cake frosted?" The two walked to the far side of the kitchen.

Why did the twins seem nervous? Calling someone by the wrong name was common enough. Most everyone had done it. How many times had he been called by one of his brothers' names? If he had a cookie for every time, he'd be fat.

Hannah spoke to Amos. "Why don't you take your suitcase out to the barn? It's going to take a few minutes to get everything on the table."

Was she trying to distract *him*?

"All right." He snagged the case and headed out to the barn. That had been strange. But then this had been a bit of a strange day. And he was surrounded by women who didn't behave or think like men. They were mysterious creatures whose sole purpose was to confuse and distract men.

He set the case on his bed and saw, out of the corner of his eye, the tabby dart in. When he turned to look, the cat dashed back out. What had scared it? He leaned to look on the other side of the potbellied stove, where the cat had run from.

A tiny kitten with its eyes still closed was lying on the ground. It raised its wobbly head and let out a small mew.

Amos picked it up. "Where has your *mutter* gone?" It seemed females of all species acted strange. He stepped out of the room and scanned the dim interior of the barn.

From the hayloft, the tabby trotted down the slanted ladder with another kitten hanging from her mouth. She ignored Amos and darted into his room. She quickly came back out and meowed at him. Then she put her paws on his leg and meowed again.

"I have your little one." He crouched down and she took the kitten from him.

He followed her into the tack room. "How many little ones do you have?"

She obviously liked the warmth of the stove for her babies. She looked from him to beside the stove and back again.

He waved his hand. "Go on. Get the others. I'm not going to make you sleep in the cold."

She darted out.

Amos snagged an unused crate, put in a layer of straw and then an old towel. By the time the *mutter* cat returned with number three, Amos had the crate with the two kittens in it next to the heat.

The tabby peered over the edge of the box, jumped in with the third kitten and lay down.

"I'll figure out how to keep the door open and stay warm later."

When he headed back to the house, all the girls sat silently at the table, hands folded in their laps. No one fluttered about. He could have waited until later to take out his suitcase. It didn't matter now. He sat next to Sarah as before.

As well as Bartholomew, Teresa and one of the twins weren't at the table. Which twin was here? She had the crease between her eyebrows, so she must be Hannah.

After the blessings, Hannah jumped right into conversation. "Now, tell me about the barn. Are you comfortable out there? If you would rather return home, I'm sure we can manage. You must miss your family."

He actually didn't miss his family as much as he'd

imagined he might, and he preferred the barn to home. Maybe leaving the community wouldn't be as hard as he anticipated. "I'm quite comfortable. *Danki.*"

Hannah continued, "We wouldn't want to keep you or put your parents in a bad position by insisting you stay."

He glanced around the table. Except for Deborah and Miriam, the younger girls paid no attention to Hannah's words. "My parents and brothers can manage quite well without me." His brothers would be running the farm soon enough without him; they'd might as well start now.

Deborah glanced from Hannah to Miriam, seemingly trying to figure out things, as well. She shook her head and went back to eating.

Miriam stared hard at him and then stabbed a cooked carrot. "If you change your mind, we'll understand."

A distraction attempt? Now more than one sister appeared to be trying to get rid of him. Eligible women were always trying to get rid of him. Women were strange indeed. "I won't. I promised Bishop Bontrager that I would work here while your *vater* is recovering." If he wasn't planning to leave altogether, he might be tempted to ask Bartholomew if he wanted to hire him on afterward to help ease his burden.

Neither Hannah nor Miriam seemed pleased with his answer. Didn't they want their *vater* to have help?

Typical strange behavior for women.

The following Monday, Deborah studied Amos as he watched Miriam. Her sister stood at the clothesline hanging the laundry. She didn't know he was observing her. And *he* didn't know that Deborah was studying him.

How fortunate for Miriam to have someone look at her the way Amos did. Maybe someday someone would regard her in such a manner. But probably not. At least not in her Amish community. The only time she'd ever been noticed was in the *Englisher* world.

Tugging her coat closed, she slipped out past the garden that had been harvested and canned last summer and fall. Spring planting was still a couple of months off.

She hurried out to the cluster of bare sycamore trees near the pond at the edge of their property. After retrieving her backpack from the tangled base of the largest tree, she headed for the meeting spot. No one would miss her. They never did. *Vater's* trip to the hospital had been proof of that.

Deborah tramped through the still-fallow field. This year would be the year this field was planted again. She came out the other side and dashed down the road. At the intersection, an idling car waited. She opened the passenger door and climbed in. Then she switched to English. "Sorry for making you wait."

The older woman pointed toward Deborah's seat belt. "I don't go anywhere until your seat belt is on."

Deborah grabbed the belt, pulled it and snapped it into place. One of the many differences between automobile travel and riding in a buggy.

The woman put her car into gear and pulled out onto the road. "I thought you might not be coming, and I was about to leave."

Deborah was glad the woman hadn't. "Thank you for waiting."

"This is certainly a strange place to be picked up. I've driven a lot of you Amish and always go to a house, not the side of the road."

"I didn't want to bother anyone." Deborah hoped the woman didn't suspect she was sneaking out. Deborah usually had another woman drive her, one who didn't ask so many questions or insinuate things.

She was relieved when the woman dropped her off at her destination. "Thank you for the ride." She paid the woman for her gas and time.

"Do you need me to come back and return you to where I picked you up?"

"No, thank you. I have a ride." Fortunately, her regular person could take her back.

She hustled away from the car before she could be further delayed and nearly ran into an *Englisher* woman with multicolored hair. "*Entschuldigen Sie*—I mean, excuse me."

The young woman stared a moment as though trying to figure out who Deborah was before she scurried away.

Deborah shrugged and ducked into the restroom of the combination gas station/convenience store to change from her plain Amish dress into a pair of jeans and a sweatshirt, and let down her hair. Where it had been twisted into place in the front, it kinked, and where it had been coiled in the back, it waved. When she wore these clothes with her hair freed, she felt like a different person. What would Amos think of her appearance? Disapprove, for sure.

She hurried to the photography studio and entered silently.

Hudson stood behind his camera, giving instructions to the model sitting on a fake rock wall in front of a backdrop featuring an old building. He had dozens of such roll-down backdrops. From urban to countryside, woodlands to deserts to mountains, all four seasons and various weather, and fantasy backdrops with mythical creatures, medieval castles, Gothic arches, waterfalls and stone stairways in the forest.

Hudson, in his late twenties, had ambitions to move to New York City and become a famous photographer. His wavy, shoulder-length blond hair and dashing good looks meant he could likely succeed on the other side of the camera, as well. When she'd first started modeling for him a year ago, she'd developed a crush on him because of all his praise and attention—two things she rarely received at home.

His assistant, Summer, was the first to see her approaching. She leaned in and spoke to Hudson in a hushed voice.

He pulled back from his camera and swung in Deborah's direction. "Debo! There you are."

When she hadn't wanted to use her real name, Hudson had dubbed her Debo. She didn't much care for it, but it was better than using Deborah and risk being discovered. Because of all the makeup and fussy hair, no Amish would guess that was her even if they ever found out. The likelihood that any of them would see her in one of these *Englisher* catalogs was slim to none. If they did, they wouldn't recognize her.

He walked over to her and gripped her shoulders. "You're my best model. Go see Lindsey and Tina for wardrobe, hair and makeup." He stared at her a little longer and was probably assessing the condition of her features today.

"What is it? Is something wrong?"

"It just amazes me how different you look from when you go into the dressing room and when you come out again. Lindsey and Tina are miracle workers. If I didn't know both women were you, I would never guess you were the same person."

Deborah counted on that. If her Amish community knew about this, she would be shunned. If the media found out she was an Amish girl modeling, they would exploit that. But Hudson and his team kept her secret, and as long as they did, she could continue to model. She wasn't hurting anyone and wasn't doing anything illegal. The money she earned would help her and her future husband buy a house and farm. She would quit as soon as someone special took interest and asked to court her.

Today's shoot was for a high-end clothing catalog. She would be transformed with makeup, and her hair would be curled and fluffed. It was fun to be pampered like this. It still gave her a chuckle at the variety of clothes *Englishers* owned and wore—different clothes for every season, every occasion and various times of day.

For her, spring and summer meant she could put away her sweater and coat and didn't have to wear shoes or stockings most of the time, going barefoot. Same dress, just fewer layers. Her biggest decision was whether to wear her green, blue or yellow dress. She wore far more outfits on a single photo shoot than she owned. Where did *Englishers* put them all? She would hate to have to wash the lot.

Once she had been rendered unrecognizable and dressed in a long, flowing summer dress she could never imagine owning, she returned to the main area of the studio.

Hudson smiled at her. "There's my favorite model." He positioned her in the shot and took a lot of pictures. Same instructions he usually gave her.

Strange to be wearing a summer dress in the middle of winter. Strange to be wearing an *Englisher* summer dress, period. She moved automatically and let her mind wander. Back to her family's farm. Was Amos still gazing at Miriam? Had her sister taken notice of his attention? Part of her hoped not.

Deborah focused on the hand snapping in front of her face.

Hudson stood less than a foot away. "You're distracted, Debo. I don't know where you were, but I need you here."

Was she distracted? *Ja.* She supposed she was. "I'm sorry." Her mind kept flittering back to Amos. Why? He wasn't her beau. Until a little over a week ago, she'd barely known he existed. Now she couldn't shake him from her thoughts. He was like a mouse in the wall, always scratching. Always capturing her attention. Always crawling into her daydreams.

She tried to push Amos from her thoughts and focused on Hudson's instructions.

After four hours of changing clothes and hairstyles and having hundreds of photos taken of her, relief washed over Deborah when the shoot was over. After changing into her own *Englisher* clothes and scrubbing off the makeup, she left the dressing room.

Hudson gathered the five models around him. "A mostly great shoot today." He gave Deborah a pointed look.

Her performance was in the part not included in the "mostly great."

"I need all of you back here tomorrow and for the rest of the week. The client wants the photos this weekend to present to his marketing department Monday."

The other models grabbed their coats and purses and headed out.

Deborah hung back. "I don't know if I can come every day."

He gave her a hard look. "Debo, I need you. You have to come."

"I'll try."

Surprisingly, she did manage to escape the farm each day, although some days were more of a challenge than others.

On Friday, Hudson praised them all for their hard work.

Deborah headed for the exit with aching feet and a tired body. Her body from constantly moving, and her feet from being shoved into impractical shoes. Her brain hurt as well from repeatedly forcing Amos out of her thoughts.

"Debo, hold up." Hudson trotted over to her. "You want to grab a cup of coffee?"

How many times in the past had she hoped for just such an invitation? She shook her head. "I'm sorry, Hudson. I need to get home."

"But we ended early. Certainly you don't have to rush off so soon."

"I have been gone too much from home this week." Not that her family noticed her absence. "And you have photos to edit for your client."

"Next Wednesday, then? I have a shoot. I'll see you then."

She shook her head again. "I need to stick around home for a while."

"If you had a phone, I could call you with opportunities."

She couldn't risk him calling their phone. That would be disastrous for her. She finally escaped, all the while her mind wandering back to Amos.

Amos looked out over the Millers' fields, which were to be plowed in the spring. He couldn't help but think of them as partly his. Since he'd already planned out the plowing and planting, they sort of felt a little like his fields. Of course, they weren't *his* fields, and he might not even be here to do the work. But if he was, he would take pride in that work.

Bartholomew appreciated everything he did around the farm, so Amos worked harder and enjoyed it so much more here than he ever had at home.

Here, even the little things he did mattered. *He* mattered. Bartholomew had never had a son to help him with all the work around the farm. How had he run this place without sons?

But on the flip side, Amos's *mutter* had been alone doing the house chores, cooking, cleaning and laundry for six men and boys through the years. How did *she* do it without help?

On the far side of one of the fields, a woman emerged from a bare stand of sycamore trees nestled next to a pond. She walked across the field he would plow in the not-too-distant future. If he was still here. Bartholomew should have his cast off by then, but he wouldn't likely be up for all the physical work yet. Maybe Amos should stay long enough to help with that.

The woman came closer and closer.

Deborah.

Where did she go all the time? She had disappeared every day this week and would be gone for hours. He was about to find out.

With her head down, she didn't see him approaching. He stepped directly into her path a few yards in front of her. She seemed to be talking to herself, but he couldn't make out all the words. Something about nothing wrong and not hurting anyone.

She kept walking with her head down. The words became clearer. "Everything will be fine. No harm done."

When it looked as though she might literally run into him, he cleared his throat.

She halted a foot away and jerked up her head. She was so startled to see him there, she took a step back and appeared to lose her balance on the uneven ground. Her arms swung out to keep herself upright.

He reached out and took hold of her upper arms to stop her from tumbling to the ground. "Whoa there."

She gasped. "I'm sorry. I didn't see you."

"Where have you been all day?"

"What? Nowhere." She tried to pull free of his grip, but he held fast.

He shook his head. "You've been somewhere. You've left every day this week and been gone for most of the day."

"I—I went for a walk."

"Where? Ohio?"

She twisted her face for a moment before his joke made sense. "We have a pond just over there by those trees. I like to sit there and watch the ducks. It's a nice place to think and be alone. You should go sometime."

"I did. Today. You weren't there."

Her self-satisfied expression fell. "I was for a while, then I walked farther."

He sensed there was more to her absence than a walk. "Where?"

"Why do you care?"

"With your *vater* laid up, I'm kind of responsible for everyone on this farm."

She rolled her eyes. "I'm fine. I can take care of myself."

How could she not understand the role of a man?

"May I go now?"

He realized he still held on to her upper arms. He didn't want to let her go but did. "I don't want you to leave the farm without telling me where you're going."

"Are you serious?"

He gave her his serious look.

She huffed and strode away.

Would she heed his request?

Where *did* she go every day? He had wanted to follow her, was tempted to. He almost did once, but he realized it was none of his business and turned around. But curiosity pushed hard on him. He still might follow her if she didn't obey. Just to see. Just to watch her from a distance. Just to know her secret.

Something inside him feared for her. Feared she would walk out across this field and never return. Feared her secret would consume them both. She was a mystery.

A mystery he was drawn to solve.

Deborah heaved a sigh of relief. She marched the rest of the way through the field, resisting the urge to run. After two weeks, Amos Burkholder already paid more attention to her comings and goings than her own family had her whole life—they never expected much from her and thought her an airhead. Fanciful. Her head full of dreams and nonsense.

Well, she did have dreams. And to prove to everyone that she was someone to be noticed, not an airhead, she'd become a church member younger than any of her older sisters at age sixteen, the same year as Miriam, who was a year and a half older than her. She'd basically skipped her *Rumspringa*. But Naomi had run away in a fit of selfishness and sent the family into a tizzy.

Miriam hadn't seemed to mind having her special day of joining church ruined, but Deborah had.

No one had congratulated her or told her how wonderful it was that she'd joined so young, that she must be the most dedicated Amish woman ever. Anything to be noticed, just once.

Instead, the whole community had gone on a search for Naomi and found her, hours later, sulking under their porch. She'd walked home by herself, having somehow slipped out of the service, probably under the guise of needing to use the bathroom. She'd stayed hidden even when she'd known people were searching for her. She'd hated that so much attention was being paid to others.

It had been the last straw for Deborah. She'd tried to get her parents' attention and had given up several times, but she'd thought joining church so young would get their attention for sure. If only for a moment. She had just about succeeded until Naomi had pulled her disappearing act. Even after their parents had scolded her younger sister, Deborah gave her a round of her own. After that, Naomi made sure to steal any attention that might be portioned out to Deborah.

Deborah decided that with Naomi always wanting the most attention, Deborah would never get her fair share, so she'd decided to take advantage of being the invisible one. She let Naomi suck up all the attention she could get from the family. Sarah, being the baby and having Down syndrome, naturally got a goodly amount of attention, as well. Joanna and Miriam both took everything in stride and seemed to almost be invisible as well, but they seemed to love it, as though it was their crowning glory to be overlooked. Always quietly in the background.

Well, that wasn't *gut* enough for Deborah. Wasn't she as important as any of the others? Wasn't she just as much in need of being noticed? Wasn't she as worthy as any of the others?

So, she took advantage of her invisibility and realized that her family never really noticed when she wasn't there. If it had been her missing that day instead of Naomi, when would her family have noticed? Certainly not as soon as they had for Naomi. It might not have been until the family was ready to leave for home in the late afternoon, instead of before the service even ended. Maybe not even until nightfall when she wasn't in her bed. Maybe never. But Hudson had noticed her.

She had experimented with being gone from the family for longer and longer periods of time, until she could be gone all day without hardly a notice. She would claim to go for a walk and be gone for hours. When she returned home, she would be told to get her head out of the clouds and keep track of time. Didn't she know they worried about her?

Worried? But they never came looking for her. When she told them that, they said she'd always been a wanderer and she always came home and she could take care of herself.

She had to admit that she had been self-sufficient from an early age. Everyone attributed it to when her *mutter* was so sick while carrying Joanna, that even at two, she somehow knew something had been wrong with *Mutter*, and it was best if she didn't cause a fuss. She'd learned to be quiet from all the shushing from adults and her three older sisters at ages four and three. They all knew to be quiet and not cause any more trouble for the family.

So, Deborah wandered farther and farther from

home. Until she ended up at the edge of a photo shoot over a year ago.

Though she tried to stay hidden, the photographer, Hudson, had seen her and said she'd be perfect for the shot. A contrast between two worlds: the outside—*Englisher*—one and the Amish one. She hadn't wanted to do it. She knew she shouldn't. Hudson told her that there would be no harm in it. That none of her Amish people would ever know.

She'd been thrilled at the idea of being special, being different. At being noticed. At no longer being invisible.

Hudson praised her and told her that she was a natural and followed direction better than most of his models. He'd paid her money for taking the pictures. He'd asked her to come to another shoot the following week. She said she couldn't, but then she found she couldn't resist and went. Soon, she participated in weekly shoots with him. After nearly two months, he asked her to change into *Englisher* clothes. She couldn't do that, could she? But she did. And she had enjoyed it. Like being a different person with each new outfit. She wasn't hurting anyone and was earning money for her future.

The clothes were always modest, but sometimes they put makeup on her. At first, she looked strange and felt out of place, but soon got used to her different appearance. None of her Amish community would recognize her when she was dressed and made-up for a shoot. She felt free and no longer invisible. She felt important. She felt like *somebody*.

But now, her absence had been noticed. Amos paid more attention than the others. Part of her liked that someone in her Amish community finally noticed, but he could become a problem if he truly did keep her from leaving for her job. It was her job. An unusual job for an Amish person, true. For her, it was a dangerous job. How ridiculous. She didn't hurt anyone. No one would hurt her. But still, it was a secret. She certainly couldn't tell Amos where she went. But how many times could she claim to go for a walk and have him still believe her? Or worse yet, ask to go with her?

If she *had been* going for a simple walk, she would welcome his company and attention. She smiled at the thought.

She sighed. That could never happen. She needed to figure something out before her next photo shoot.

Chapter Four

When Deborah rolled out of bed Monday morning, she was actually kind of pleased to be able to stay home and not have a photo shoot demanding her attention. Last week had worn her out. Between the sneaking off, traipsing through the lumpy field and posing just so over and over, every muscle in her body had tensed up. Even muscles she hadn't used for any of those tasks. Just the stress made everything taut.

But there was no stress today. She could help out her sisters and *Mutter*, or slip away and relax at the pond. Maybe she would do a little of both.

After breakfast, *Vater* sat in the living room with his leg propped up, and Amos had gone outside to work in the barn. The lumber he'd ordered with *Vater's* permission and gratitude had arrived late on Saturday. Today, he would start his repairs on the hayloft.

Mutter scurried into the kitchen with her coat on. She scanned her daughters. "I'm going to Sister Bethany's Fabric Shoppe. Your *vater* needs a new shirt, and I want to start a new quilt." Her gaze settled solidly on Deborah. "Would you like to come with me?"

Deborah couldn't believe it. As she stood a little

taller to speak, she opened her mouth, but before any words could come out, Naomi stepped in front of her.

"I want to go. Can I go with you, *Mutter*?"

"Of course. You can all go. Get your coats."

Hannah and Lydia exchanged glances and identical tilts of their heads.

Sarah clapped her hands. "Yeah. I want to go."

"I'll stay here and start preparations for lunch," Joanna said.

"I'll stay, as well," Lydia said. "Sarah, do you want to help me make a cake? I'll let you lick the bowl."

Sarah clapped her hands again. "Oh, *ja*. I want to lick the bowl."

Mutter had invited Deborah, and now half of her sisters were going.

Hannah, Miriam and Naomi quickly bundled into their coats. Hannah would drive and *Mutter* would sit up front with her. That would leave Deborah to sit in the back with Miriam and Naomi. Miriam was always a pleasure to be with. But Naomi?

Mutter looked directly at Deborah. "You don't have your coat on. Aren't you coming?"

Naomi made a face at Deborah from behind *Mutter's* shoulder.

Lydia put a hand on Deborah's shoulder. "I could use your help with the cake."

Deborah knew her sister didn't, but said, "*Ja*, I'll stay and help."

Mutter smiled at her middlemost daughter. "You are such a *gut* girl."

Deborah smiled back. Her *mutter's* brief attention was somehow worth not going.

Naomi's expression turned smug before she stepped out the kitchen door ahead of everyone. Why her next-to-the-youngest sister insisted on being spiteful didn't make sense to Deborah.

"Mutter?" Deborah asked. "Could you get me some fabric for a quilt, as well?"

"Of course, dear." With that, the foursome left.

Lydia didn't move from Deborah's side but stared out the window at the top of the door. She looked a little troubled, then spoke softly. *"Danki* for not making a fuss about staying. I figured Hannah would have her hands full with Naomi along. Why our sister has chosen you to clash with, I don't know."

It was nice to know that at least one other person in the family noticed Naomi's ill temper toward her. "I do my best to stay out of her way."

"You do it very well. I'm pleased you take the high road."

Maybe that was why no one minded Deborah being gone. Naomi behaved better in her absence. "What do you need me to do?"

Sarah pulled on Lydia's arm. "I wanna lick the cake bowl."

Lydia gave Deborah a helpless look. "See if *Vater* needs anything. We'll start the cake." Her sister allowed their youngest sister to drag her to the cupboard with the mixing bowls.

Deborah liked feeling useful. With her *mutter* and half of her sisters gone, there would be something for her to do. She stopped short in the middle of the living room. *Vater* lay fast asleep, pushed back in the recliner. She returned to the kitchen. *"Vater's* sleeping. What can I do?"

Lydia glanced around. "I think we have it all covered. *Danki* for asking."

Even with half of the women gone, she wasn't needed. "Why don't you read a book or something?"

Deborah didn't want to read a book. She'd been eager to help. Movement outside caught her attention.

Amos helped *Mutter* and her sisters into the big black buggy.

His kindness and thoughtfulness made Deborah want to be near him. "I'm going to take Amos a cup of coffee and a leftover biscuit from breakfast."

Lydia set a large mixing bowl on the table in front of Sarah and handed their youngest sister a wooden spoon. "That would be very nice. I'm sure he would appreciate it."

Deborah hoped so. She snatched her coat, swung it on and fastened it up the front.

Lydia handed Deborah a mug of steaming coffee and the remaining breakfast biscuit. "You're so thoughtful."

If her sister only knew her kindness was an excuse to go see their handsome helper. As she stepped outside, the buggy had just turned onto the road. She hurried to the barn. "Amos?"

He stepped from a horse stall and smiled when he saw her. "*Hallo*, Deborah. What brings you out here?"

His greeting tingled her insides. She held out the offerings. "I brought you coffee and the last biscuit."

He leaned the pitchfork up against the wall and removed his work gloves before he took the biscuit and coffee. "*Danki*. This is quite a treat."

"A treat? It's just a biscuit and coffee."

"Ah, but I come from a farm with all men and one woman. There were never leftovers, so extra food was unheard-of. My brothers and I gobbled up every last crumb our *mutter* prepared." He took a sizable bite. Before long, the beverage and food were gone. "*Danki.*

Now that I'm fed, I'll be able to continue my work throughout the morning."

"Are you going to work on the hayloft today?"

"*Ja.* This is a *gut* time, before plowing and planting."

"I'll help you."

His brown eyes stared at her and blinked several times. "I can't allow that. Carpentry is man's work."

She took a deep breath and huffed it out. "Didn't we already go over this? One man, lots of women." She pointed to herself. "Done a little carpentry from time to time. Helped plow and plant. And taken care of the livestock. I even once helped my *vater* fix and grease a buggy wheel."

He shook his head. "I just can't picture you wielding a tool."

Deborah grabbed a framing hammer from where tools hung on the wall. She felt the weight of it in her hand and then rotated her wrist, turning the implement in a circle.

Amos chuckled.

"You think me incapable?"

"*Ne.* I'm thinking you are probably quite capable. I'm grateful for your assistance. While I was waiting for the wood to be delivered, I moved the hay back away from the edge using both the attached ladder and the A-frame one. I removed some of the near boards I could reach from the loft. Your *vater* approved and bought wood for the whole floor to be rebuilt. I could use your help in handing the boards up to me. Do you know where your *vater* keeps his work gloves? I wouldn't want you to get any slivers of wood."

That had been too easy to get him to agree. She'd thought she would have to do a lot more cajoling to get him to consent. She went over to a plastic tub on the floor and popped off the top. After taking out her favorite pale green pair, she snapped the lid closed to keep bugs and critters out of the gloves.

After two and a half hours of hauling up boards and nailing them in place, Deborah was more tired than she'd been in a long time. She was also more satisfied with her work than she'd been in a long time. There was something so gratifying about accomplishing a task like this. Not like modeling, where she sat there and posed this way and that. It wasn't fulfilling. Not like this had been.

Miriam entered the barn. "My goodness, you've made quite a bit of progress."

Amos nodded toward Deborah where she stood on one of the two ladders. "Your sister helped. I wouldn't be nearly as far along without her."

"Deborah can be a very hard worker."

Not a glowing compliment, but at least it wasn't negative.

Deborah felt bad that she was spending time with the man who was interested in Miriam. It reminded Deborah that she often wasn't around to help with the work. She wasn't usually needed anyway, and she shouldn't feel bad working with Amos, because she'd done nothing wrong or inappropriate. Miriam could have offered to help him.

"She's been very helpful." Amos shot Deborah an appreciative glance.

Deborah's insides tingled at his encouraging look.

"We all strive to do our part." Miriam shifted her gaze from Amos to Deborah. "I just came out to let you know that lunch will be ready in about fifteen minutes, if you want to get washed up."

"Danki," Deborah said at the same time Amos did.

"Bitte." Miriam left without so much as a second glance at Amos. So, hopefully her sister wasn't any more interested in him than he seemed to be in her.

Deborah scurried down her ladder as Amos climbed down his. She certainly was hungry and knew a delicious meal awaited. She removed her gloves, as did Amos. Deborah grabbed both pairs and tucked them safely inside the plastic bin.

"Just a second." Amos headed back for the ladder. "I want to bring down the nail pouch, so I don't forget to refill it before we go back up." He climbed up.

We. He'd said *we.* So he *wanted* her to continue to help him. She smiled. She definitely wanted to continue to help him, as well. It gave her a chance to spend time with him and be useful.

"Got it." He backed down the ladder. "Ouch!" He jerked his right hand away from the ladder.

Deborah stepped closer. "What happened?"

"Splinter. I should have been more careful." He jumped the rest of the way to the ground and tossed the nail bag onto the stack of lumber.

"Let me see." Deborah grabbed his hand and turned it palm up. The realization that she was holding a man's hand—a man who wasn't a family member—sent a jolt up her arm. She still wasn't doing anything wrong. She was merely helping someone who was helping her family.

He scratched at his palm with his fingernail. "I can take care of it."

"It's your dominant hand. It'll be easier if I do it." She released him. "Move over to the brighter light of the doorway." He obeyed.

Deborah took a slow, deep breath to calm her fluttering insides and grabbed the red-and-white first-aid kit off the tool wall. Popping it open, she set the kit on the end of the pile of boards and removed the tweezers.

Once her fickle insides were wrestled under control, she cupped her hand around his and lifted the end of the large sliver with the tip of the tweezers, pinching it. "This is going to hurt."

"Pull it out fast and get it over with."

"Okay." She yanked it free as she spoke the word.

He sucked in a breath through gritted teeth but didn't move his hand, not even a twitch.

It took all her strength to focus on the sliver and not on holding his warm, strong hand in hers. *Keep your breathing natural.* She picked out a couple of more small ones, then dabbed the abrasions with an alcohol wipe. "There. That should do it. Are there any others? I can't see any." When he didn't answer, she looked up.

He stared down at her with a strange expression on his face.

Her question came out a little soft. "Did I get them all?" Leaving her hand cupped around the bottom of his, she continued to stare up at him. That same strange feeling she'd had when he'd knocked her out of the way of the falling board more than a week ago wrapped around her like a gentle hug.

After a moment, he nodded but didn't pull his hand away. "We should go wash up for lunch. We don't want to keep the others waiting."

This time, she nodded but didn't move until a loud motorcycle raced by on the road. She drew in a quick breath, breaking the moment and retrieving her hand. "I'll put the first-aid kit away."

He cleared his throat and dropped his hand to his side. "*Danki*. It feels better already."

His praise caressed her like a long-awaited, warm spring breeze.

Tuesday, again she had another pleasant day helping Amos with the hayloft. But Wednesday was a different matter entirely. She was expected at the studio for a shoot. She needed to slip away undetected by Amos. A part of her wanted to stay and work beside him again even though they had finished the hayloft floor. She'd told Hudson she didn't know if she would be able to make it, but he was counting on her. And if she was going to be honest with herself, she missed modeling and Hudson's praise.

However, slipping away had been easier than she'd thought it would be. Amos drove *Vater* to Dr. Kathleen's to check his leg. *Mutter* went as well, along with Hannah and Naomi, so Deborah had a *gut* excuse not to go. The buggy was full with *Vater's* leg needing to be propped up.

Deborah had been able to stroll at a leisurely pace through the field as she had done before Amos arrived. She caught her ride and reached the studio early. She hurried inside.

Hudson stood with Summer, Tina and Lindsey over what appeared to be concept drawings. Which meant today's shoot wouldn't be for some boring clothing catalog.

Deborah liked these shoots best. She could be more free and have fun. "Am I the first model here?"

Four pairs of eyes turned toward her.

Hudson stepped away from the group. "Yes. You're early." He sounded pleased.

Was that because she was early or just because she

showed up after saying she might not? It didn't matter. She was here and glad about it. She joined them at the table to look at the printouts of various period dresses and multiple backgrounds.

Deborah picked up a paper with a royal blue velvet gown. "I call dibs on this one. First come, first serve."

Hudson waved his arm over the table. "You get to wear them all."

"What about the other girls? Are we all going to take turns wearing each dress?"

"Not exactly. You're the only model today."

She set down the paper. "Is everyone else sick?"

"No. I need only one model today. And since I can't call you to cancel, I canceled the others."

So did that mean Deborah had been a last resort? Hudson didn't seem to be upset that she was his model today. She had told Hudson from the beginning she didn't have a telephone number. Though her *vater* did, she technically didn't. She couldn't risk him calling. She would never be able to explain receiving a call from an *Englisher*. And an *Englisher* man, no less.

Deborah would stand in front of either one of the different pull-down backdrops or a green screen in the assorted outfits, and Hudson would put her in various backgrounds, mostly outdoors ones. These shots would likely be for book covers. "So, you're shooting covers today."

"Yes. I have several custom-ordered for specific books. The others I'll put on my website to sell."

She posed in a Victorian dress, a medieval gown and a gypsy outfit, as well as others. Her favorite was the flowy, gauzy lavender fantasy dress with sparkly accents.

"Gaze off into the distance as though you see someone you're glad to meet." Hudson snapped multiple pictures as he spoke. "Turn on the fan."

A gentle breeze played with her loose hair. What would Amos think if he could see her?

"Good. I like that distressed look."

She was modeling only until she found someone to marry, and that wasn't likely to be anytime soon.

"I'll put you in a meadow, on a high castle wall, and even give you wings."

Amos would think her silly, foolish and worthy to be shunned. Her insides twisted at the thought of him being so disappointed in her.

She spun and faced the camera. "I'm sorry. I need to go."

"But we still have more outfits to shoot."

"Call in one of the other models." She hurried to the dressing room. It had been a mistake to come.

Amos stood in the barn, greasing a buggy wheel. He'd noticed it squeaking a little on the trip to the local Amish doctor's.

He had his usual supervisor—the gray tabby—who watched him work in and around the barn. He'd learned the cat's name was Sissy. Amos had cut out a small section of the tack room door at the bottom for the cat to come and go. By the time he'd gone to bed that first night, Sissy had brought two more kittens, for a total of five. He enjoyed having them as roommates. When Sissy got tired of her kittens, she would curl up on his cot.

Once again, he stepped away from his work on the buggy wheel to go outside and look beyond the barn toward the field Deborah often disappeared through. He'd thought she might help him. She said she'd greased a buggy wheel before, but she'd taken advantage of him being gone to take her *vater* to have his leg checked and had left without permission or telling anyone where she'd gone.

He'd been a bit breathless on Monday when Deborah had removed his wood sliver. Not from the pain but from having a woman holding his hand. Not holding his hand like they were courting, but nonetheless, her touch had affected him. At first, it had briefly reminded him of when his *mutter* had removed slivers from his hands when he was a boy, but it had quickly turned into something different. Something more. Something he wanted to repeat. Could Deborah be different from the other Amish girls who had disappointed him? Part of him hoped so. But why hope for anything when he was leaving? It wouldn't matter.

Today, she wasn't here to tend to any wounds he might incur. She had slipped away while he was gone. He'd become complacent because she'd been helping him the past two days. He should have insisted she come to the doctor's with them. He'd forgotten she *was* different from other Amish girls. Not content to stay around the farm. She had a restlessness about her. What was it that caused her to feel the need to always wander off?

He'd already trekked out to the pond in case she had simply gone there as she said she often did, but she was nowhere in sight. Though he hadn't really expected to find her there, disappointment that she wasn't had stabbed at him. He would have to wait until she returned, and then he would keep an even closer eye on her from now on. He shouldn't allow himself to get tangled up with thoughts of her. Thoughts that would likely lead to heartbreak again.

When he returned inside to the buggy, Jacob was leaning against it. "You are a difficult man to track down."

Amos looked back toward the door opening. None of the Millers were around to take notice of his cousin.

Jacob pushed away from the buggy. "I made sure I wasn't seen."

That was a relief. "It's *gut* to see you. What are you doing here?"

"Looking for you. You weren't easy to find. I was on the road near your family's farm every day for nearly a week and didn't see you once. Then I remembered where you said you were working. Are you staying here?"

"*Ja*. Bartholomew broke his leg. I'm helping out on his farm while he's laid up. It's fairly light work, being winter. I did replace his rotting hayloft floor." He pointed above him. "That's how he injured himself."

"You appear to be enjoying yourself."

"The work is *gut*." And he slept like a contented man because of it.

Jacob's mouth hitched up on one side. "Or is it because you have your eye on one of his daughters? Are you looking for a *frau* while you're here?"

Part of Amos *was* looking for an Amish *frau*. Was it because he wanted one? Or because it was expected of him? Or because he wanted to believe a *gut* Amish woman could fall in love with him? On the other hand, Jacob was here to help Amos leave the Amish. Amos wasn't sure what he wanted anymore. "*Ne*. I don't think I'm ready to marry yet." He needed to figure out where he belonged first. Here, in his plain world, which might include Deborah, or out there, in the fancy one without her.

"Do you still want to leave?"

"*Ja*. I think I do."

Jacob pulled a cell phone and cord from his jacket pocket. "Then I brought this for you. Have you used one before?"

Amos nodded. "On *Rumspringa*." He hesitated before taking the forbidden device. This was a step down a path away from Deborah.

"Make sure to keep it charged. I'll text you with a meeting time and place. I've put it on Silent, so you'll need to check it each day for messages and text back that you received it. I'll contact you with a time and place for next week. Will you still be here or at your parents' farm?"

"Here." Amos shifted his gaze from the phone to his cousin. "But I don't know if next week will work. Bartholomew still needs my help."

"He wouldn't have any trouble finding someone else. Maybe even one of your brothers."

Jacob was right, but Amos didn't want anyone else taking his place here. This was his place. At least for the time being. "I made a promise to him." When he was no longer needed here, it would be easier to leave. Being on the Millers' farm had already been a small step in breaking ties with his family.

Jacob studied him for a moment. "Do you truly want to leave?"

"*Ja, ja.* I do." No sense in getting even more attached to this family.

His cousin narrowed his eyes. "All right. I'll be in touch to see how things are going." He shuffled his feet. "How are my *mutter* and *vater* and my brothers and sisters?"

"They are doing well. They miss you."

Jacob laughed. "I know they didn't say that. That would be frowned upon."

"I can tell by their guarded speech when they talk about their children and their worried expressions. And you are prayed for at church." When Amos left, he would be included in the unnamed lost members who left the Amish faith, along with Jacob, the bishop's granddaughter and a few others.

Amos walked Jacob to the barn door opening and peered out into the yard to make sure no one was there. The pair stepped outside. He wished his cousin farewell and watched him until he made it to the road.

Rubbing a hand across the back of his neck, he tried to sort out his thoughts. It would be easier to break ties with his community when he wasn't needed here. But for now, he *was* needed. He returned to the barn to finish greasing the buggy wheel.

"Who was that *Englisher*?"

He looked up and saw Deborah strolled toward him.

"Who?"

"The man who just left."

Should he make up a story, tell her the *Englisher* was lost and had asked for directions?

"He's the same man you spoke with at the hospital, isn't he?"

She'd seen him then? He'd thought he'd sneaked away unnoticed. Now she would think less of him. He decided to go with the truth. "That was Jacob. My cousin."

"Oh. Is he still on *Rumspringa*?"

"Ne."

Her big, beautiful green eyes widened. "He left the church?"

"Six months ago."

"What was he doing here?"

"Asking about his family."

"But he turned his back on them when he left."

"He still cares about them. Just because someone leaves doesn't mean they no longer believe in *Gott*."

"Is he going to come back?"

"I doubt it." He didn't want to talk about his cousin anymore. "When your parents and I came back from the doctor's, you were gone. Where did you go?"

Her eyes widened again, and she looked away. "For a walk. I went to the—"

"Don't say the pond, because I checked there."

She gave him a steady stare. "Well, I *did* go there first. Then I walked farther. As my family says—" she put on a silly expression "—I'm fanciful with my head full of daydreams and nonsense."

He narrowed his eyes. "You aren't nearly as out of touch with things as you would like your family to believe. I believe you're quite smart and intuitive."

Her facade changed to a mix of shock and…pleasure? "You think I'm…smart?"

"Why wouldn't I? You seem smart to me and quite capable."

She straightened and stood a little taller.

But before she could distract him further, he said, "I told you that you need to tell me where you're going."

She gave him a tight smile. "You weren't here." She turned toward the buggy. "You want me to help you with finishing up?" She was changing the subject.

He should press the issue, but he didn't want to argue with her, didn't want to scare her away. He wanted things to be pleasant between them. "I would like that. Next time, tell someone where you're going. I know you don't understand or believe it, but I do feel responsible for everyone here while your *vater* is recuperating."

"But you're not. I can take care of myself."

"Sometimes your family may not notice you, but I do."

She gifted him with a sweet smile that made his brain a little fuzzy.

Chapter Five

Deborah sat at the kitchen table almost a week and a half later, poking her finger into a flat of potting soil and dropping in vegetable seeds. It would give their kitchen garden a head start. Lots of celery for the impending weddings this fall.

Amos had planted himself firmly in her mind with his declaration that he noticed her. Though his attention to her whereabouts hampered her ability to escape when she needed to leave, it was nice to have someone aware of her. What kind of an excuse could she give to go outside to see him, if only for a minute or two?

Hannah strolled in. "*Mutter* needs thread."

Deborah's ears perked up. "Is she going to Sister Bethany's Fabric Shoppe again?"

Hannah shook her head. "She wants to stay with *Vater*. Lydia, would you mind going for her?"

"I'll go." Deborah jumped to her feet and brushed dirt from her hands. She had missed out on a trip to the fabric shop the last time, and *Mutter* had forgotten to get her fabric for a quilt. Thanks to her modeling job, Deborah had money to buy her own fabric.

Lydia smiled. "That settles it. Deborah and I will go."

Sarah jumped up and down. "I wanna go. I wanna go."

Lydia pulled a stiff smile and tilted her head. Her sister didn't like to make waves. Deborah could tell she was trying to decide whom she was going to disappoint. Deborah or Sarah. Lydia was a peacekeeper.

Deborah took the decision out of her hands. She put her hand on Sarah's shoulder. "We would love for you to come with us."

Lydia gave her an appreciative smile.

Sarah was most generally always a joy to be around, more so than Naomi. Why couldn't Naomi just be nice to her? Deborah had never done anything to her. Maybe she would be better when she grew up a little more.

"I'll get my shopping bag, and then I'll go see about hitching up the buggy." Deborah ran upstairs and grabbed some of her money she had tucked away and her canvas shopping tote. When she came back down, she swung on her coat.

"*Danki*, Deborah," Lydia said. "I'll get Sarah ready."

"It's not a problem." She headed to the barn.

Amos was there, working diligently. Today, mucking out a stall. Deborah never saw him slacking off in his duties. He was always *doing* something. Sissy, one of their barn cats, watched his every move.

"You are such a *gut* Amish."

He faced her with a smile, and her heart soared. "You are *gut*, too."

"I'm not all that *gut*." If he knew about her secret life, he wouldn't say such things.

He leaned on the shovel handle. "Did you need me for something?"

"*Ne*. I'm just getting the buggy ready. Lydia, Sarah and I are going to Sister Bethany's Fabric Shoppe."

"I'll help you."

"You don't have to." But she hoped he did.

"I want to. I'm done here." He pushed the full wheelbarrow out of the way. "I'll get the harness. Would you get Floyd from his stall?"

"Sure."

Floyd was a large gray-and-black draft horse. A gentle giant. He greeted her with a nicker and tucked his head over her shoulder, pulling her close for a hug.

She wrapped her arms around his beefy neck. "I'm glad to see you, too."

"He really likes you."

Deborah turned.

Amos stood with his arms folded, his hip leaning against the stall frame and a crooked smile on his face. "I've never seen a horse so friendly before."

"Floyd has been in our family for a long time. I believe he's special."

With the bridge of his nose, the large draft horse nudged her back, which was equivalent to someone shoving her quite forcefully. Deborah careened forward several steps to try to keep her balance. But it wasn't going to do any *gut*. Momentum and gravity were going to land her face-first on the ground.

Amos jumped forward and caught her in his arms, keeping her from landing in a heap in the straw. "Whoa."

The silly horse did that on purpose. But why?

She stared up at Amos.

And stared.

And stared.

Did he realize he was holding her? She should back away, but truthfully, her knees had lost their ability to hold her up.

This needed to stop happening—standing so close

to him and gazing at him like he could ever mean anything to her. And *touching*. *Ja*, always innocently, but nevertheless, touching.

He'd come with intentions toward her sister Miriam. Hadn't he? But he never spent any time with her, and Miriam never manipulated events to be near him. She seemed content to wait for him to come to her. Maybe Deborah could help them. That thought caused a dull ache to form in her chest.

She kept staring.

But he was staring, too.

She cleared her throat and forced strength back into her jellied legs. "I'll lead Floyd out."

He cleared his throat, too. "*Ja*, right. I have the harness ready." He released her and backed away, then turned and disappeared.

She spun back to the gray-and-black draft horse, shook her finger at him and spoke in a low voice. "You did that on purpose. Behave yourself."

The big ol' lug whinnied, bobbing his head up and down.

"Are you laughing at me?"

The horse bobbed his head again.

She grabbed his rope from the wall, then tossed the loop over his head and around his neck. "You need to learn some manners."

The big draft horse hooked his chin over her shoulder and pulled her in for another hug.

Poor thing thought she was mad at him. "I forgive you. But if you do it again…I won't mind." She led him out to where Amos stood between the buggy shafts. She maneuvered Floyd around and backed him into place. Whether hitching up a horse or rebuilding a hayloft floor, being near Amos made her insides dance.

Soon the buggy was ready, and Lydia and Sarah came out to where the buggy was parked in front of the house.

Sarah let go of Lydia's hand, ran to Amos and threw her arms around his waist. "Amos!"

He patted her on the back. "*Gut* to see you, Sarah."

Lydia touched Sarah on the shoulder. "Leave Amos alone."

Sarah stepped backward and latched onto his hand.

"Sarah, what were you told about running up to people and hugging them?"

"But I know him. He's not a stranger." She pulled him toward the buggy. "You coming with us."

Lydia put her hands on her hips. "Sarah, let him go."

Sarah's bottom lip pushed out as she released him, and she plopped down on the ground. "I want Amos to come with us!"

Deborah did, too, but couldn't say so. *Please let Sarah get her way.*

This was typical behavior for Sarah. She loved everyone and thought of everyone as her friend. When she got scolded, she often threw a tantrum.

Amos knelt in front of her. "I would love to go with you, but you need to ask nicely, *ja*?"

His patience with her Down syndrome sister warmed Deborah's heart.

"You come with us…please?"

"It would be my pleasure." When Sarah tilted her head, he added, "*Ja*, I will go."

He was going! Deborah's heart skipped a beat.

Sarah jumped to her feet and pulled him toward the buggy door. She climbed in the front. Assuming Amos would drive, that left the back for Deborah and Lydia. Though disappointed at first, it did afford her the vantage point of watching his profile as he drove without it being awkward or anyone noticing what she was doing.

Amos looked back over his shoulder. "Are you two doing all right back there?"

She and Lydia nodded.

Soon they arrived at Sister Bethany's Fabric Shoppe, a small building to the side of the main house on Bethany and her sister's parents' property. Deborah and her two sisters piled out, and Amos took care of Floyd and the buggy.

Lydia stopped Sarah on the porch. "Remember not to touch everything. If you want to look at something, ask me first."

Sarah nodded briskly, and they all went inside.

Besides fabric and sewing notions, Bethany and her sister Rosemary had finished quilts for sale, completed clothes, wooden toys, Amish dolls with clothes and a small variety of jarred canned goods and cooking utensils. A little bit of everything, most of it made by people in their district.

Deborah headed straight for the solid colored fabrics. Bethany and Rosemary had fabric already cut in common lengths. It was time Deborah had a new dress, as well as started a quilt for when she got married—*if* she got married. What color would Amos like? She chose a pink fabric for a nice spring dress and various other colors for a quilt.

Sarah tugged on Deborah's arm.

"What is it, sweetie?"

"Deborah." Sarah pushed an Amish romance novel into her stomach. "Deborah."

Deborah had forgotten about the Amish novels the sisters carried in the store. Though Deborah already had one checked out from the library that she was reading, she took Sarah's offering anyway. *"Danki." Amish Identity* by Mary Rosenberg. At least the model on the cover was dressed accurately. She'd seen books where the model actually had the cape dress on backward. This one looked very authentic. In fact, she had a dress this same col – Deborah gasped. *She* was the model on the book's cover!

At the very first photo shoot she'd stumbled upon, Hudson had said he would create book covers with her image. She just never imagined her picture would ever make the cover of any book. Ever! But here she was. Fortunately, it didn't expose her full face. She'd been too shy in the beginning to look at the camera. But the side view of her looking down at a black-eyed Susan was still unmistakably her.

"Deborah," Sarah said again.

Her baby sister wasn't just calling her name, she'd recognized her on the cover.

"Shh." Deborah put her finger to her lips.

Purchased books were often passed around the community. Not this one. Deborah stuffed it into her shopping bag. Then she hurried to the shelf of books and thumbed through the others. Another book by the same author, but no others with Deborah on the cover. She sighed with relief.

Sarah pulled at Deborah's cloth shopping bag. "Deborah."

Deborah crouched and put her finger to her lips again. "Shh. Let's not tell anyone."

"I want the book!" Sarah said in a louder-than-necessary voice.

Deborah glanced around, but no one looked their way. Then she grabbed a carved wooden cat and held it toward her littlest sister. "Would you like me to buy you this kitty?"

Sarah's almond-shaped eyes widened. "*Ja.* I want the kitty." And with that, Sarah was both distracted and pacified.

Bethany rang up her sale, including the fabric, book and wooden cat. She held the novel in her hand. "Have you read this author before?"

Deborah shook her head, hoping Bethany didn't look too closely at the cover.

"I hear this author's more accurate with the Amish details than most of these writers. I don't know that I believe she's actually an Amish woman. No real Amish woman would write a novel."

Well, the cover was more accurate. A little too accurate. If Deborah modeled when no other Amish would, she supposed anything was possible. She wanted to snatch the book from Bethany's hands and stuff it back into her bag.

"You'll have to tell us how you like it." Bethany finally released it.

"You're buying a book." Amos stood right beside her.

Deborah put her hand over her head on the cover. "*Ja.* These can be entertaining. It's fun to pick out the inaccuracies and to get an idea of how *Englishers* view us." She pushed it toward the opening of her cloth shopping bag hanging on her arm, but the corner kept getting caught on the top edge and the handles.

"Careful," Bethany said. "You don't want to damage the cover."

Oh, but she *did* want to damage the cover. She wanted to make it unrecognizable. She couldn't let Amos—or anyone else, for that matter—identify her. Finally, the book cooperated and dropped safely to the bottom. Deborah quickly shoved her fabric on top of it and paid.

Amos frowned at her. "Your face is red. Are you feeling all right?"

She nodded quickly. "It's just a little warm in here. I'll wait in the buggy." She hurried out into the cold and took a deep breath.

That was close.

Chapter Six

A̲t breakfast the next morning, Amos wiped the last of the gravy off his plate with a biscuit. He was going to get fat if he kept eating like this, but the Miller ladies cooked so well, and there was always plenty of food for him to eat until he was full. He wasn't used to there being leftovers, but there generally was.

Bartholomew took a swig of his coffee. "You'll leave right after breakfast."

Amos swallowed hard to get his last bite down around the rising lump in his throat. "I don't think I should go. You're still in a cast." A new cast, in *Ordnung*-approved black. He'd had to color the foot portion of his former bright green one that showed below his pant leg with a black marker.

Bartholomew smiled. "Though you've been a huge help and put my mind at ease, we will survive one day and night without you. Don't get me wrong. I deeply appreciate all you've done around here. My new hayloft floor looks quite sturdy, but it's important for you to visit your family. I'm sure they miss you."

Amos wasn't so sure about that. Work tended to be light around the Burkholder farm, and even lighter in the wintertime. "I will head off soon." Though he *was* reluctant. He glanced at Deborah.

She piped up. "*Vater?* It's quite a ways and cold out. Maybe one of us could drive him home so it doesn't take him all day."

"Fine idea. Did you have someone in mind?"

Amos liked the idea of a long ride with Deborah.

"What about Miriam?" Deborah seemed pleased with herself.

He was unexpectedly disappointed, even though he supposed a ride with Miriam would be quite pleasant, as well.

Miriam sneezed. "I think I'm coming down with a cold. It wouldn't be a *gut* idea to be in a cold buggy for hours. Why don't you go, Deborah?"

Bartholomew reached for his crutches. His shoulder had healed well enough in the last little while for him to use them on a limited basis. "Then it's settled. Deborah, you go. Take the trap."

The open, two-wheeled buggy would be appropriate, since it would just be the two of them.

"I wanna go," Sarah pleaded.

Teresa patted her youngest daughter's arm. "Not this time, dear. You stay here with me. We can bake some cookies."

"Cookies!"

Amos pushed away from the table. "I'll hitch up the buggy."

Deborah smiled at him. "I'll be out in a few minutes."

He had the buggy hitched by the time Deborah came out lugging a heavy, thick canvas bag. He took it from her. "What's in here?"

"Warmed bricks for our feet and a warm quilt to cover our legs."

He situated the bricks on the floor and helped her in. "I'm sorry Miriam couldn't go."

He wasn't. But was Deborah truly sorry she had to go?

He put the buggy into motion and pulled up on the road. "When this was your idea, why did you suggest your sister go? Do you not like my company?"

"*Ne*, that's not it at all. I like your company *very* much. I mean, I enjoy time with you. Oh, I don't know what I'm saying."

She was cute when she was flustered. What had caused her to sputter? Him? "So, why your sister?"

"When you first arrived, I thought you were interested in her. Weren't you? Aren't you?"

He shrugged. "Maybe at first."

"But not anymore?"

"*Ne.*" Someone else occupied his thoughts even if he didn't want her to.

The pleasant drive to the other side of the district took over two hours. As Amos drove into the yard, he felt like a foreigner returning home. This was only the third time he'd seen his family since he'd gone to work at the Miller farm. The other two times had been at the biweekly church services.

Bartholomew had talked Amos into this overnight trip home. He hadn't wanted to go. But he could protest only so much before Bartholomew would have suspected he didn't want to go home. This was going to be a long few hours until bed and then again in the morning. Hopefully, his family wouldn't sense his reluctance to be home. He would return to the Millers' with them after church tomorrow.

He parked the buggy out front. "Come in and meet my parents," he suggested as he helped Deborah down.

His *mutter* rushed outside into the cold without a

coat. "Amos!" She hugged him, then turned to Deborah. "You must be one of the Miller girls. I'm sorry, but I don't know your family well enough to know which one you are."

"*Mutter*, this is Deborah."

"I'm pleased to meet you." His *mutter* hugged Deborah, as well. "I'm Karen."

"I'm pleased to meet you, too, Karen. Or rather, meet you again."

"I think I remember you have older sisters who are twins, then some other sisters and the sweet baby is Sarah."

"That's right."

From the barn came his *vater* and two brothers, who each shook his hand in greeting.

Amos gritted his teeth. "*Vater*, this is Deborah Miller." He turned to her. "My *vater*, Joseph. This is Daniel and Titus."

Mutter waved her hand in the air. "Come in out of the cold for a slice of pie and a cup of hot tea," his *mutter* said to Deborah. "It will be nice to have some female company."

Daniel elbowed Amos. "I assume you're going to be courting Deborah. But what about the others? Are any of the others being courted?"

His brother's question surprised Amos. He hadn't thought him interested yet. "The two oldest are being courted." He wouldn't say that they would be engaged this fall, as that was the family's business to announce after the engagements were official. "As far as I know Miriam isn't being courted, nor Joanna, but she's still a little young." Amos wouldn't say that he wasn't courting Deborah, nor did he plan to court her. There were plenty of other young ladies for his brother to consider.

Vater clasped Amos on the shoulder, causing him to tense. "*Mutter*, you and Deborah go on inside. I need to talk to Amos for a minute."

Amos watched Deborah disappear into the house.

"Daniel, Titus, go finish the work in the barn." *Vater* waved his hand for them to leave.

Why couldn't Amos leave, as well? "What do you need to talk to me about?"

"You've had some time to think while at the Millers'. Have you made up your mind what job you want to pursue?"

Ja, Amos had done a lot of thinking, but not about what his *vater* referred to. "It's a big decision." Bigger than his *vater* realized.

"I'm sorry this farm isn't big enough to divide three ways, but don't let that stop you from making this decision. Don't put it off."

Amos wasn't putting off going into the *Englisher* world. Not really. True, he likely could have left by now, but the Millers really did need help. And he'd said he would help. He was a man of his word. When Jacob said to go, Amos would find someone else to help the Millers and be gone. He could do that. Couldn't he? Something twisted inside him.

Vater and Amos joined *Mutter* and Deborah inside. Amos set the bricks on the stove to warm up before Deborah made the drive back home. He supposed he could have driven himself with the Millers' buggy and returned it tomorrow when he went to church. Why hadn't he thought of that before? Maybe because a part of him wanted to spend time with Deborah.

The following morning, Amos's desire to get to church churned inside him like a whirlwind. His family had all said that they had missed him and included him as though he hadn't been gone for a month. As *gut* as it was to visit his family, seeing Deborah—all the Millers—would make him happy. He looked forward to returning home with them.

When his family arrived at the host home, he immediately scanned the crowd outside for the Millers. He didn't find any of them. They must not have arrived yet.

He studied each buggy as it pulled into the Beilers' yard. He and his brothers had shown up early to help set up. Church was due to start in a few minutes. Where were the Millers? He knew he shouldn't have left them. With Bartholomew still recovering, they needed a man around. They needed him.

Then at last, a final buggy rolled down the road with a horse clopping briskly in front of it. Floyd.

He met the buggy where it parked.

Hannah sat at the reins.

"I'm sorry," Amos said. "I should have come by your place to help you all."

Hannah smiled. "That wouldn't have likely gotten us here any faster. Our issues were beyond anyone's control."

He could have at least helped. "You all head inside, and I'll take care of Floyd."

Everyone piled out, and Sarah wrapped her chubby arms around his waist. "I missed you. Don't ever go away again."

He patted the girl's back. "It couldn't be helped, and I won't be able to stay on your farm forever. I'll have to leave sometime." He sought out a glance from Deborah, and she graciously gave him one. Had she missed him? He felt drawn to her. What was it about her? There were things about her he didn't know. There was more to her than the normal Amish-piety exterior. Could she be the forthright Amish woman he'd been looking for?

"I'll help Amos," Deborah said.

His heart cheered.

The others tromped off. Hannah had her arm looped through her *mutter's* and seemed to be whispering in her ear.

Amos worked on unhooking the harness from the buggy. "Where's Miriam?"

Deborah's smile slipped a little. "She's at home. She was too sick to come."

"I'm sorry to hear that." What had changed Deborah's mood? He'd only asked about— "I only asked because she hadn't been feeling well, not because I'm interested in her. You believe me, don't you?"

She gazed at him with that wistful almost smile that made his heart do funny things. *"Ja."*

The rest of the Millers filed inside while Amos and Deborah tended to Floyd and turned him out with the other horses in the field.

He escorted Deborah inside. She went up to sit with her sisters and her *mutter*, and he sat in the back with his brothers. Deborah sat on the outer end, almost as though she didn't belong with the family. He understood the feeling of not quite belonging in one's own family, or in the community.

After the service, Lydia left with Dr. Kathleen to look in on Miriam.

At the end of the afternoon, Amos hitched the horse back up and drove the Millers home.

He found he felt more comfortable with Deborah's family than his own. They had different expectations of him and were grateful for all his work, instead of thinking of him as less capable because he was the youngest.

Later in the evening, Amos dug out the cell phone from where he'd stashed it under his cot.

The kittens, now about five weeks old, climbed out of their box, up the side of the quilt that hung down to the floor and onto the cot. He petted the three that faced him and meowed. They were very cute, and he enjoyed watching them change from day to day. One of the kittens leaped from the cot to his thigh and climbed up.

Once the kitten had settled himself on Amos's shoulder, he pressed a button on the phone to light it up. A text from Jacob waited. He clicked the message open.

How are you doing? Will have a place for you to stay soon.

Amos hit Reply. Doing well. Soon will be fine. Still needed at the Mi—

"Hallo," a female voice said behind him.

Amos fumbled the phone and then shoved it inside the front of his shirt before turning around. "Deborah." He should have closed the door to his small living quarters.

"I wish we had a bigger space for you than this." Deborah stood in the doorway.

"This is fine. It takes less to heat."

"It does seem toasty in there. Maybe a little too toasty. Your face is red."

He didn't doubt his face looked flaming hot, but it wasn't from the heat. He'd almost been caught using an unauthorized device.

"How are the kittens doing?" She plucked one from his shoulder.

"They're getting very energetic and don't want to stay in their box anymore." He sucked in a breath as another kitten suddenly attached itself to his back and proceeded to climb.

When the kitten appeared over his shoulder, Deborah laughed. "Do they do that a lot?"

Her laugh sent a thrill through him, making the needlelike claws worth it.

He thinned his lips and nodded. "I tried to stop them, but..." He shrugged. Like his growing feelings for the girl standing before him.

After Deborah left, Amos pulled the cell phone back out of his shirt. He hoped Deborah hadn't noticed it there. He finished his text to his cousin and pressed Send.

If he was caught using an unapproved cell phone, he could be shunned. Then how would he help the Millers? He stashed the phone back under his cot, farther than he had before. What if someone came in here and found it? No one usually entered his quarters, that he knew of. Everyone respected this as his area.

But still, he needed to be careful.

Deborah would never understand and would be the first one to shun him.

The thought of her never talking to him again made his heart hurt.

Chapter Seven

After a shoot the following week, Deborah headed back across the field to the pond in the stand of trees. Once the fields were planted and growing, she wouldn't be so noticeable tromping across them. She stashed her pack among the sycamore trees and covered it with dry leaves. They were getting pretty shredded and small, more like confetti these days. When she prepared to make a dash for home, she stopped short and gasped. *"Mutter!"*

Busted!

She looked in one direction then the other. No one else was around.

Mutter walked back and forth and in circles at the edge of the pond.

Deborah hurried over to her. "Wh-what are you doing here?" Had *Mutter* seen her stow her change of clothes?

Mutter turned her gaze on Deborah with a confused glaze in her eyes. "I don't know. Where am I?" She had the hem of her apron between her fingers and was pulling at it as though she was trying to pick something off it.

What was wrong with her? Was *Mutter* playing some sort of game? Had she seen Deborah and wanted her to confess? "Um, the pond? I was just taking a walk."

"A walk." *Mutter* blinked several times, then her face lit up in recognition. "Deborah." She looked around. "What are we doing out here?"

Deborah knew what she was doing, but it was a little scary that *Mutter* didn't know why she was here. Didn't she know why she came? Did she realize Deborah had come from a different direction than from the house?

Mutter rubbed the sleeves of her dress.

That was when Deborah realized *Mutter* wasn't wearing a coat. She took her *mutter's* hands. Ice-cold. She quickly removed her own coat and manipulated her *mutter's* arms into the sleeves. Though she didn't cooperate, Deborah prevailed and fastened the buttons down the front. What had her *mutter* been doing out here in the cold without her coat?

"Thank you, dear. You're so sweet."

Deborah wrapped her arm around her and guided her in the direction of the house. Goose bumps rose on Deborah's arms. The early-spring sun wasn't strong enough to warm the air much.

Halfway between the pond and the house, Amos met up with them. "What are you doing out in the cold without a coat?"

"I gave mine to my *mutter*."

Amos squinted at *Mutter* but didn't comment on the coat. "Let's get you two back where it's warm." He shucked off his coat and put it on Deborah. His warmth enveloped her.

She resisted the urge to release a contented sigh. "What about you? Won't you get cold?"

He shook his head. "I'll be fine. It's not far."

Far enough to get cold. But she didn't argue because she was cold, and his coat was so warm.

The trio walked in silence and entered through the kitchen side door.

"Mutter." Hannah tried to keep her tone light, but Deborah could hear the concern in it. "There you are. I didn't know you went outside."

"She was out by the pond." Deborah rubbed her hands together.

Hannah and Lydia exchanged worried glances.

Then Hannah spoke in a level but firm voice. "Joanna, take Naomi and Sarah into the other room."

Naomi opened her mouth to protest but was silenced with a stern look from Hannah. The three shuffled out.

Miriam swung on her coat, grabbed the milking bucket and crossed to Amos. "Would you walk me out to the barn?"

The late-afternoon milking gave Miriam an excuse to leave the house and take Amos with her. Deborah recognized the chore as an excuse. Why was Miriam deciding now to show an interest in Amos? He wasn't even interested in her anymore. But he hadn't put up a fuss and allowed Miriam to easily take him away. A little too easily. Jealousy reared up inside her. She tamped it down.

Amos glanced back over his shoulder on his way out.

Chores and romance aside, something more important was going on. Something unpleasant. Deborah turned to her older twin sisters. "Why was *Mutter* outside without a coat? She was freezing."

Lydia's weak giggle wasn't convincing. "Oh, *Mutter* is fine. She goes out all the time without her coat. One would think she was an Eskimo. You don't need to worry about her."

Vater hobbled into the kitchen on his crutches. "You found her." He put his arm around *Mutter's* shoulder. "Let's get you warmed up."

Hannah took Deborah's coat off *Mutter* and handed it to Deborah. "You should probably return Amos's coat to him. We wouldn't want him to get sick."

From under the sink, Lydia pulled out the tin washbasin and set it on the floor in front of a chair. They would put *Mutter's* feet in warm water and give her some hot tea.

Vater gave Deborah a pointed look. "*Ja*, Deborah. Amos will be needing his coat."

So many questions festered on her tongue. The three of them obviously knew something about *Mutter*. Deborah didn't know exactly how to phrase those questions, so she left. She would ask later.

When she got out to the barn, the sound of milk swishing into a bucket met her ears. The cow stall blocked her view of Miriam. Was Amos with her? Deborah hoped not. She breathed a sigh of relief when she found him in the tack room, where his cot was. The kittens tumbled around on the floor of the toasty room. "I brought you your coat." She reluctantly took it off and put on her own. His warmth was gone. She missed it.

"*Danki.*" He took it and put it on. "Can I ask you a question?"

Oh, dear. He was going to ask where she'd gone today. "I guess so."

He narrowed his eyes. "What's wrong with your *mutter*?"

Deborah squinted back at him. "Nothing is wrong with her."

"*Ne.* I didn't mean that to sound disrespectful."

"Well, it did."

"What I meant is that she's not like other women. She's different. Forgetful."

"Aren't we all forgetful from time to time? Haven't you ever gone into another room and forgotten why you were there?" Deborah knew she did on occasion.

"This is different. This goes beyond those little things. She's called me Bartholomew at least three times and David a few times. I know Bartholomew is your *vater*. But who's David?"

Her *mutter's* brother. "Haven't you ever accidently called someone by the wrong name? Hasn't your *mutter* called you by one of your brothers' names? Most all *mutters* do."

"This is different. I can tell she thinks I *am* David. Who *is* he?"

"Her brother. He was older than her by ten years. He died when she was fifteen."

"She mistook me for David when I first arrived. She stands in the yard like she doesn't know why she's there. Then one moment she looks at me as though she'd never seen me before, then the next she suddenly remembers me."

Her *mutter* had looked at Deborah like that. Deborah had thought that with so many daughters, her *mutter* got confused about which girls in the community were hers, and that memory challenges came with age.

Amos faced Deborah squarely. "That's not normal."

Her *mutter* wasn't normal? She'd just chalked it up to her *mutter* being a little quirky and ditzy. She felt overlooked and that no one truly cared whether Deborah was around or not. Now that she thought about it, other *mutters* didn't seem that way. With Deborah being gone during the day so much this past year, she hadn't noticed her *mutter* declining.

Amos put a hand on her shoulder. Deborah's concern for her *mutter* numbed her response to his touch. He seemed so sincere, so caring. "I'm afraid she might get hurt or lost or worse. What would have happened if you hadn't found her?"

Her *mutter* did seem worse than usual. Especially since *Vater's* injury.

"Do you think my *vater's* injury could have anything to do with it?"

"It was pretty stressful for her. Would be for anyone to have a loved one injured."

Deborah didn't like to think of her *mutter* as anything less than 100 percent. She hadn't really thought that there was anything seriously wrong with her. Deborah would watch her *mutter* closely and stay at her side for the next couple of days.

What she saw, and the conclusion she came to, caused her stomach to pinch and twist.

Deborah sat with her *vater* on the porch. *"Vater?"*

"Ja."

"Have you noticed that *Mutter* is a bit…forgetful?"

He chuckled. "Aren't we all?"

Just what Deborah had said to Amos when she was defensive. *"Ne.* I mean more so than the rest of us. She… she's not like the rest of us. I think something might be wrong."

"Wrong?" His voice rose. "There is nothing wrong with your *mutter*. Don't say things like that." *Vater* struggled to his feet, one foot still in a cast. He awkwardly jammed the crutches under his arms. It made his show of angry haste almost comical.

Deborah would have laughed if not for the seriousness of her *mutter's*…condition? Did she have a *condition*? She definitely had something.

Deborah watched her *mutter* for two more days, and her concerns grew with each passing day.

She tried to approach her older sisters with her concerns, but they told her to leave it be.

Did everyone know something was off with *Mutter*? No, not all of her sisters. Her three older ones did—and for a lot longer than Deborah had—but no one would talk to her about it. Except Amos, and he wasn't family. Nor did he know any more than she did.

What was she going to do?

Chapter Eight

Amos reread his cousin's text message from last night. Jacob would pick him up on the far edge of the Millers' field away from any houses. He wanted to show Amos where hc would be living when he left the community. Make Amos more comfortable with the idea of leaving.

He wasn't comfortable with the thought of leaving at all, but neither was he with staying. He *had* become comfortable at the Millers'.

If he wasn't forced to return to his parents' farm, he would seriously consider remaining Amish as well as single. Amish was what he knew. Leaving had seemed to become necessary to go into the *Englisher* world to work. So why bother returning to the Amish one? No *gut* could come from having a foot in each world. He would end up preferring one and resenting the other.

Amos tucked the cell phone into his coat pocket and peered out the barn door. None of the Miller girls or their parents were in sight. He could escape undetected. He strode briskly across the field, hoping no one came out of the house until he was on the other side of the sycamore trees by the pond. Though they had no leaves yet, their trunks would hide his progress through the other side of the field.

This was the same direction Deborah left by. When she "went to the pond," did she keep on going this way? Did she feel the same guilt he did? Not likely. She was just going for a walk. Unlike him sneaking off.

He'd meant to question her yesterday about where she'd gone, but he'd been distracted by Teresa wandering and Deborah without a coat.

Something was going on with Teresa, and he suspected that Bartholomew and the older girls knew about it. But not being a family member, they weren't likely to confide in him.

He passed by the pond and glanced at the log he'd shared with Deborah. He'd enjoyed their walk and would like to do so again. What beyond the pond drew her away from the house so often? He saw nothing of interest, just more fields. Did she visit a friend? Or meet up with a young man? That unsettled him. It shouldn't. He shouldn't be thinking of taking walks with Deborah at all when he didn't plan to stay in the community. And yet, his mind—or his heart—managed to repeatedly sneak off in that direction.

At the road, Jacob waited, leaning against an old blue pickup truck. He spoke in English. "I thought you might not come."

Amos responded in *Deutsch*. "I texted you that I would."

Jacob continued in English. "Yeah, but I know how things can come up." He patted the side of the truck. "How do you like my ride?"

His cousin sounded like a fancy outsider. After only six months? Would Amos sound like that soon? "It's nice." He supposed it was nice, but didn't know vehicles, or particularly care about them. Sure, he'd driven cars on *Rumspringa*. Driven fast, but knew, for him, they were always temporary. Another thing he had been wrong about.

Jacob shook his head. "Out here, you'll need to speak English."

For some reason, Amos didn't want to. "I will when we get to wherever we're going." He saw no reason to do so now. Jacob understood *Deutsch*.

Jacob pushed away from his truck. "Jump in." He climbed into the driver's seat.

Amos made his way around the other side and got in. A part of him bristled that this was *wrong*. He shouldn't be doing this, but he wasn't actually doing anything *wrong*. There was nothing *wrong* with getting a ride from an outsider. Being with a former Amish would be frowned upon, and if discovered, Amos would be admonished, though being in a vehicle wasn't technically *wrong*. But going against the *Ordnung* and his promise when he joined the church *was* wrong. Where he was going and why—*that* was *wrong*. His actions today would be more than frowned upon. He would be shunned. None of that would matter once he left. Except Deborah. He would miss her. The thought of not seeing her made his chest ache.

His cousin put the truck into motion. "You'll like Donita and Frank. They're a sweet couple. They left the Amish life twenty years ago. Half of their ten children went back, the other half stayed fancy. Now they help other Amish who wish to leave. You'll live with them until you find a job and can get your own apartment."

Amos hadn't given much thought about what he'd actually be doing once on the outside. He'd pictured it a bit like *Rumspringa*—just hanging out with other people, not putting down permanent roots like a job and an apartment. He was woefully unprepared for this. His instinct had been to leave. "I don't know how to do those things." Would there be any jobs on farms? That was the only work he knew. And carpentry. All Amish knew how to build. But with so many men being forced to work in the *Englisher* world, would there even be any jobs available for him?

"They'll help you with everything. Getting a driver's license, finding a car or truck to buy and locating a place to live. You could stay with me, except there are already five of us in a little two-bedroom apartment. Maybe we could find something together, just the two of us."

Amos liked the idea of rooming with his cousin. It would make the move easier.

"I don't know if I want a car." However, his Pennsylvania driver's license, which he'd gotten on *Rumspringa*, was still valid for a few more months. Leaving the community didn't mean he had to throw the whole *Ordnung* out the window. He just wanted to see if it was the right place for him.

"You'll need one to get around."

"I can walk."

"In the winter?"

His cousin had grown soft.

"I'll manage, and spring's here." Barely. He needed to think about plowing. He needed to make sure the Millers' plow and tractor were in *gut* condition. If they were anything like the rest of the farm, they likely needed some work.

Jacob chuckled. "You'll change once you've been out here for a while."

Did he want to change? A part of him didn't. One of the reasons he was speaking *Deutsch* while Jacob spoke

English. At the same time, he didn't want to remain as he was on his *vater's* farm. He didn't feel as though he fit in there. Hadn't *Gott* made it clear the Amish life wasn't for him? Or else Esther would have married him, and he would have stayed in Pennsylvania. He would have land to work.

Before long, Jacob pulled into a driveway on the edge of town. The house was a modest size. Probably had been an Amish home at one time. The sizable yard nestled up to a field.

"Do they have a working farm?" he asked in *Deutsch*. He could work on their farm. That made him smile.

His cousin shook his head and spoke in English. "No, they have only the house. The fields belong to an Amish family." He put the truck into Park, turned off the engine and got out.

Amos hesitated before doing the same.

A man who looked to be about sixty stepped out onto the porch and was dressed in typical *Englisher* clothes—nothing fancy, just a red-plaid flannel shirt and jeans. "Come on in. Donita has some hot chocolate and cookies waiting for you, boys." That must be Frank. He spoke in English with no hint of his former Amish life.

Amos was probably going to like this man. He followed Frank and Jacob inside. The aromas of chocolate and cinnamon wrapped around Amos like a warm blanket. Made him feel comfortable and at home. From the delectable smells, he could mistake this for an Amish home.

The house was similar to an Amish one, but with pictures scattered on the walls and shelves, as well as some useless knickknacks. But for the most part, the interior was simple.

Donita's smile lit her whole face. "Welcome. Please, sit down." She had no accent either.

Had these people actually been Amish?

Amos grumbled inside. He was going to like her, too. What was his problem? Wasn't it *gut* that he liked them? He sat on a glider-rocker and accepted the steaming mug of liquid bliss with marshmallows and a sprinkle of cinnamon.

Donita's eyes twinkled. "This is how Jacob liked his cocoa when he lived with us."

That made sense as to why she'd made it perfectly. Amos had loved his aunt's made-from-scratch hot chocolate. The cinnamon had been the perfect touch.

Amos spoke English out of respect for his host and hostess. "Thank you." He took an offered chocolate chip cookie. His favorite.

After the hot chocolate and cookies, Frank stood. "Let me show you the room you'll be in when you come to stay with us."

Amos stood, as did Jacob. Frank climbed the stairs first, followed by Amos, and Jacob tagged on at the end.

Frank knocked on the first door on the left. "Jesse's at work, but I like to knock anyway." He opened the door to a small room with a twin bed, nightstand, dresser and small desk.

Simple. Functional. Inviting.

Frank stepped aside. "This will be your room when you come. It may be small but you'll have it to yourself. Jesse will be moving out at the end of the week. We found a family at church who will rent him a room."

"Why doesn't he just stay here and rent from you?"

"We provide the first landing, so to speak. We feel led to assist with the transition and prepare you for a life on your own. We'll help you learn how the world outside the Amish community works."

Jacob jumped in. "On the surface, it seems like it would be simple to just move to the *Englisher* world, but when you've grown up having all your decisions made for you, like we have, it's not as simple as moving into town. It's a huge adjustment."

Frank nodded. "Donita and I are here to make your transition easier. We have a weekly Bible study here for any former Amish who want to come. We have quite a crowd on Tuesday nights."

Amos liked the idea of having people to guide him. "This is very nice. I'm sure living here will be *gut*."

Frank motioned down the hall. "This is the bathroom. You'll be sharing it with five to eight others. All depending on how many we have at any one time. If you decide to come before Jesse leaves or even stay right now, we have a cot we can set up in one of the rooms."

The thought of staying right now and not seeing Deborah again made his stomach tighten. "I can't stay right now. I'm helping out an injured farmer. He has all daughters. He doesn't have anyone to do his farmwork while he heals."

"All daughters?" Frank smiled. "I understand."

It wasn't like that, but it didn't matter if he thought Amos was angling to court one of them. Because he wasn't.

Jacob led the way back downstairs and shook Frank's hand. "It was good seeing you. I'll keep you posted about this one." He squeezed Amos's shoulder. "We need to get going."

Amos shook the older man's hand. "Thank you for showing me around and explaining things." He turned to Donita, who sat, typing on her laptop computer.

"Thank you for the hot chocolate and cookies. They were very *gut*."

"You're welcome. I look forward to seeing you again."

Unfortunately, he was definitely going to like these people. He hadn't realized until now that he'd secretly hoped to not like them, because it would have given him a reason *not* to live in the outside world. He'd thought he *wanted* to like them. Was afraid he wouldn't, which would mean his transition to the *Englisher* world would be harder. But he did like this nice couple. They were eager to make his transition trouble-free, so it would be easy for him to leave one life for another. Nothing to stop him now.

Deborah popped into his head. Would she understand why he was doing this? Of all people, he thought she might, but he couldn't tell her.

Amos headed outside with his cousin. He needed to get back before he was missed. He got into his cousin's truck.

Jacob pulled out of the driveway. "So, did you like them?"

For some reason, he was loathe to answer, but did so honestly. "*Ja*, I did. I really did."

"You sound surprised."

He was. He had anticipated *not* liking them. How could he like people who'd turned their backs on their Amish faith? But wasn't that exactly what he was planning? "I know why you brought me here."

Jacob turned onto the country road leading to the drop-off spot. "Why?"

"You wanted me to get to know Frank and Donita so I'll be more comfortable leaving."

"It's human nature to resist new things. I sense you're changing your mind. Ever since you started working on the Millers' farm, you've been weakening in your resolve."

"Not true. It's just that I'm needed there. As soon as Bartholomew's back on his feet and strong enough, I'll leave."

"Are you sure?"

"Ja." But that wasn't true. If his cousin had been pushing this the week before Bartholomew got injured, Amos would have already been gone, and the bishop would have asked someone else to help the Millers. Who would it have been? His brother Daniel? Daniel certainly was keen on finding out if any of the Miller girls were available to be courted. Would he be interested in Deborah? *Ne.* Daniel wasn't right for Deborah. Maybe Miriam.

His cousin pulled to the side of the road, where he'd picked up Amos. Amos climbed out of Jacob's truck.

"I'll text you next week to let you know how things are going. We don't want to put this off too long, or you'll come up with all sorts of reasons not to do it."

Amos nodded and shut the door. He could sense reasons already forming in the deep corners of his mind, and that was where he would keep them. He *needed* to leave his Amish life.

Jacob drove off, and Amos headed across the field.

Halfway between the pond and the house, a girl ran toward him. Sarah. Her arms flailed as she stumbled over the uneven ground. Her almond-shaped eyes were wider than normal. "Amos! Amos!"

He quickened his pace. When he reached her, he lowered onto one knee. "What is it, Sarah? What's wrong?" Was it Bartholomew? Teresa? Deborah?

Sarah hugged him. "You were gone. I got scared of you."

Was that all? He was gone? He looked beyond the girl to Deborah sauntering toward them. "Sarah. Let Amos go."

Sarah shook her head against his shoulder. "*Ne*. I don't ever want him to leave again."

Deborah knelt next to her little sister and patted her back. "It's all right. He's here now. Let him go."

Sarah pulled back but kept a grip on his shoulders. "You not go away again!"

Deborah took a deep breath.

He sensed she was going to admonish her sister, so he spoke up. "I already told you that I can't promise to never go away. This isn't my farm. When your *vater* is all healed up, he won't need me any longer. I'll have to leave then."

"*Ne, ne, ne!* You have to stay. I won't like you if you leave."

"I'm sorry. I'll come visit." But he couldn't very well do that if he was shunned. This little one might be the most upset of all when he was gone. Would Deborah be upset at all?

Sarah slapped her hands on the top of his shoulders. "I don't like you!" She ran for the house.

"Sarah! Come back here and apologize," Deborah called.

But the girl wouldn't be stopped.

Amos stood and held out his hand for Deborah. Interesting that Sarah was upset that he'd left but hadn't made a fuss when Deborah went missing for most of a day.

Deborah took his offered assistance and stood.

Her bare hand in his warmed him all over. He didn't want to let go, and she didn't seem eager to retrieve her hand even after holding it was no longer necessary. He stared down at her. He should let her go.

And not just her hand.

She stared up at him. "I— We missed you. Where did you go? No one knew where you went or knew anything about you being gone."

That spoiled the moment. He pulled his hand away and started walking again toward the house. "Um... I went for a walk." Wasn't that what Deborah always told him?

Deborah fell into step beside him. "A walk? To the pond, no doubt."

Her tone told him she suspected he went farther than just the pond. "I wanted to see what was in that direction that fascinates you so much. You take a lot of walks that way." *Gut.* He could turn this back to her being missing yesterday. He hadn't gotten to ask her where *she* went. His questions for her had been preempted by her *mutter* wandering in the field. "I didn't get to ask you yesterday, where you had gone. You forgot to tell me before you left."

"Oh, yeah. Oops. Sorry."

He waited, but she didn't say anything more. "So, where *did* you go?"

"Does it really matter now? I'm back."

"*Ja*, it does." Mostly because he was curious.

"I went for a walk." She picked up her pace.

At the edge of the yard, he did something he shouldn't. He took hold of her arm. "We need to talk about this." He guided her toward the barn.

Once inside, she turned and folded her arms. She looked upset. Upset with him.

He wanted to let this go. He wanted to make her happy. Make her smile. But he couldn't drop this. "I need to know where you went yesterday." She opened her mouth, but before she spoke he continued, "And don't say for a walk. I need to know specifically where you were."

"Why can you go for a 'walk' and not report to anyone, but I can't?"

"Because I'm a m—"

"A man. That's not a reason. It's an excuse. You tell me where you went today on your 'walk,' and I'll tell you where I went on mine."

He couldn't do that. She wouldn't understand. He took a slow breath. "What if something happened to you?"

"I'm here. I'm safe. End of story."

"If I thought it was the end of you disappearing, I would drop this, but I'm not confident you won't wander off unannounced. If something happened to you, no one would know where you were."

She stared at him a long while before answering. "Nothing happened to me. What if something had happened to you?"

"Why do you keep turning everything back on me?"

"Am I? Maybe *I* was worried that you disappeared without telling anyone. You saw how upset Sarah was."

"Sarah? Is she the only one who was upset?" He hoped Deborah had missed him.

She straightened. "Well…we were all concerned for you."

Why did he get the feeling she was hiding something? Because he was? Did all of his suspicions about Deborah stem from his own guilt? No wonder she didn't want to tell him when he treated her not much better than a criminal. What should he do? He didn't want to make her feel bad, but he felt responsible for her.

One word popped into his mind. *Trust.*

He supposed he did trust Deborah. He really hadn't thought about it one way or the other. Why would he? He didn't *not* trust her, but he'd been treating her as though he didn't.

"I fear I've been treating you like a child, like I don't trust you. I want you to know that I do trust you. From now on, you don't have to tell me *where* you're going, but I do need to know you're safe. Though I would appreciate knowing where you are." He waited, but she didn't say anything. "Don't you have something to say?"

"Like what?"

Seriously? She was supposed to be so impressed that she confessed her secret to him.

That didn't happen.

"Like where you go all the time."

She chewed on her bottom lip, then spoke. "I go… into town. To visit a friend…in need."

Finally. "That wasn't so hard, was it?"

"So where did you escape to?"

He was a man and didn't owe a woman an explanation of his whereabouts. Even so, he wanted to tell Deborah the truth but couldn't. She wouldn't understand what it was like for a man. Now that she'd told him where she went, he couldn't turn the questioning back on her. "I had hoped to ascertain where you went all the time." He'd tried to figure that out while he walked across the field to meet Jacob.

Of course, *she* would have a noble reason for leaving all the time. He should have guessed. Now that he knew she was helping someone, what excuse could he have for singling her out to talk to her so often?

Living on a farm with all women and girls except

Bartholomew Miller was vastly different than home with all men and boys except his *mutter*.

There, it had been sensible, ordered and predictable.

Here, chaos reigned. Unbeknownst to him *how* it was possible, this bedlam worked.

Deborah lay in bed in the dark, staring up at the ceiling. She felt like a heel. She hadn't lied directly to Amos. Not really. She had just omitted what kind of "need" Hudson had. He *needed* models. Could he do a shoot without her? Of course, but he was technically still in need.

She'd kept trying to get Amos to talk about where he had gone, as benign as it probably was, to distract him from where she'd been. But he was like the squirrels who kept going after the food in the bird feeder. They never gave up, and Amos wouldn't give up asking her.

She needed to be more careful about returning. She had focused on getting away and hadn't worried about when she came back home. How could she return without him seeing her? The problem was, after she'd been gone all day, he was probably on the lookout for her.

Maybe she could have her ride drop her off at a different place so she could look as though she was coming from somewhere else. But how many different places could she be picked up from and dropped off at?

Across the room, her sister breathed slow and deep.

Too bad Amos wasn't still interested in Miriam, then he would be too distracted by her to notice whether Deborah was around or not.

Her heart tightened at the thought of all of the attention he would pay to her sister.

Ne. Miriam wasn't the answer.

As Amos had said, it was only until *Vater* was

healed, and then Amos would leave their farm. She didn't like thinking about him no longer being here. Not seeing him every day.

Maybe she wouldn't need to sneak away many more times while he was here. She had a shoot next week, but maybe after that, she could tell Hudson that she couldn't make any other shoots for a while.

That was a better solution.

She rolled over and tried to force sleep to come.

Chapter Nine

Deborah waited until everyone was busy elsewhere to use the telephone in the house by the front door. Even though they had one, no one could use it without *Vater's* permission. The chances he would grant permission for this call didn't exist. She never had much cause to use the phone. Whom would she call that she couldn't visit in person?

She picked up the slim gold-colored phone from the small table and slipped out onto the front porch with it, closing the door against the cord but not latching it. Glancing around the yard for any signs of Amos, she carefully removed the receiver as though someone might hear the nonexistent sound. She pressed the numbers for Dr. Kathleen's clinic, hoping the beeps of the buttons didn't carry inside, and leaned toward the door to listen for anyone coming.

Nine months ago, Kathleen Yoder had returned after being gone from the community for fourteen years. She'd done what no other Amish person had. She had gone to college and become a doctor. Then she'd returned and was now the community's doctor.

She didn't call herself Dr. Yoder, as an *Englisher*

would have. Or now that she was married, she didn't go by Dr. Lambright. She went by Dr. Kathleen. Some people simply just called her Kathleen. She didn't seem to mind. The community had been slow to accept her as a doctor, but most people had come around.

One ring, then a second came through the line.

"*Hallo.* Dr. Kathleen's medical clinic. Jessica speaking. How may I help you?"

"*Hallo,* Jessica. This is Deborah Miller."

Jessica's voice brightened. "Hi, Deborah. How are you and your family?"

"We're all fine. Well, mostly. That's why I'm calling."

"Are you ill? The doctor has an opening after lunch if you would like to come in then."

"That would be great."

"I'll just write your name in her appointment book."

"Oh. It's not for me. It's for my *mutter.*"

After a pause, Jessica said in her same cheerful tone, "All right. I've got her name written down. What does she need to see the doctor about?"

How was Deborah supposed to answer that? "I don't really know. That's why I want Dr. Kathleen to see her."

"What are her symptoms?"

"Um. Forgetfulness. She gets confused sometimes. But only sometimes."

"Have her come in after lunch, and Dr. Kathleen will see her." No need for a specific time, as with outside doctors. Everyone had lunch right at noon, so after that, the travel distance determined the approximate time. And no need to worry if you were a little—or a lot— late. The doctor worked in everyone.

Deborah hung up, hoping she was doing the right thing. If no one in the family would talk to her about what was going on with *Mutter,* then she needed a professional's opinion. What if *Mutter* wandered off and got hurt?

Now the question was how to get her *mutter* to Dr. Kathleen without anyone stopping her. Or asking her what she was doing.

She slipped back inside, but before she could set the telephone back on the small table, it rang.

Deborah jumped, sucked in a breath and looked around. Their phone rarely rang. Dare she answer it? Of course, there wasn't anything wrong with that. She picked up the receiver.

It was Jessica. "Dr. Kathleen said that she would like to check on your *vater*, so she'll come out to your place after lunch."

"Ne!" No one else could know about taking her *mutter* to see the doctor. They would try to stop her. "Never mind. We're fine." She clunked the receiver into the cradle.

"Who was that?"

Deborah swung around to face her *vater* leaning on his crutches. "Um." She glanced at the phone. "Jessica... at Dr. Kathleen's clinic. She...wanted to know how *you* were doing."

"Did you tell her I'm doing well?"

She gave a noncommittal nod.

Vater hobbled away.

She slumped against the door. That was close.

After lunch, a buggy pulled into the driveway. When Dr. Kathleen stepped out, Deborah's stomach lurched.

Ne, ne, ne!

She'd told Jessica *not* to have the doctor come. Oh, this was terrible. Bad, very bad. She needed to stop Dr. Kathleen before she spoke to anyone.

She ran outside to intercept the doctor, but Hannah and *Mutter* got to her first.

And *Vater* called out from his place on the porch. "*Hallo*, Kathleen."

Too late now. Her *vater* was one of those who called the doctor by her first name alone.

How was Deborah going to keep Dr. Kathleen from saying anything about her call regarding her *mutter*?

Amos approached and took hold of the horse's bridle. "Do you want me to unharness him?"

"*Ne*," Dr. Kathleen said. "I won't be very long."

He gave a quick nod. "I'll take him to the water trough and secure him there."

"*Danki*."

Amos's attention shifted away from everyone and everything else and turned to Deborah.

She bit her bottom lip to control the smile that threatened to bubble over. How could she feel so silly just because he looked at her?

He tilted his head toward the barn. "You want to help me?"

Ja, but she couldn't. "I want to hear what the doctor has to say." *And keep her from saying something she shouldn't.*

Dr. Kathleen climbed the steps onto the porch. "*Hallo*, Bartholomew. How are you doing today?"

"I'm doing well. What brings you here?"

Deborah dragged her attention from Amos and willed the doctor not to say. "Oh, she was probably just driving by and decided to stop in, for a visit, all by chance, no planning, just happened."

Her *vater* and sister stared at her.

Dr. Kathleen smiled, then looked at *Vater*. "I came

to see how you're doing. I wanted to check your leg and that shoulder to see how they're healing."

Deborah sighed, but the doctor could still let it slip that Deborah had called.

Vater glanced at Deborah. "Deborah said you'd called. You didn't have to come all this way."

Mutter opened the screen door. "Why don't we all go inside? I'll make some hot tea." She seemed normal today.

Maybe Deborah had acted rashly. Maybe there was nothing wrong with *Mutter*. Maybe Deborah had imagined the whole thing.

Everyone trudged inside. Everyone except Deborah.

The doctor hadn't said anything. Yet. But when she was through examining *Vater*, she would certainly turn her attention to *Mutter*.

Deborah better get inside to keep that from happening. The rest of the family had gathered in the living room, as well. A crowd would make it harder to steer the conversation, or to stop Dr. Kathleen from saying something Deborah hoped she wouldn't. Deborah stuck the tip of her index fingernail between her teeth.

Mutter and Hannah brought out two plates of old-time cinnamon jumbo cookies to feed everyone, as well as a tray full of steaming mugs.

When *Mutter* sat, she waved a hand toward Deborah. "Don't bite your nails."

Deborah lowered her hand into her lap. Her being repeatedly missing from the family went unnoticed, but this, her *mutter* noticed. She snatched a mug of tea and a cookie from the coffee table and slouched back into the straight-backed chair.

Sure enough, once Dr. Kathleen said *Vater* was recovering well with no unforeseen problems, she turned to *Mutter* and struck up a conversation.

To most people, it probably sounded like two Amish women having a typical conversation. But Deborah could hear the small hesitations from her *mutter* and little things that were wrong in what she said. But to the unaware person who didn't know *Mutter* well and didn't live with her, she sounded like any other Amish woman. But she wasn't.

Dr. Kathleen held up her half-eaten cookie. "These are delicious. Did you make them?"

Mutter said *ja* at the same time Hannah said that she'd made them. Then her sister corrected her statement to say they both had.

Mutter shifted on the sofa to face Hannah, who was next to her. "Martha, I made these myself."

Oh, dear. That was *Mutter's* sister's name. *Mutter* wasn't all right. What would happen now?

Not realizing her mistake, *Mutter* continued, "You were never *gut* at making these. They always turn out flat. But you make the best cakes. Mine never turn out very *gut*."

Vater struggled to his feet. "Well, we won't keep you, Kathleen."

Had the doctor noticed that *Mutter* had called Hannah by the wrong name? Would she say anything? Maybe the doctor didn't know them well enough to have realized the wrong name was used. *Vater* had noticed and was eager to have the doctor leave.

Thankfully, the doctor hadn't said anything about Deborah calling her clinic to try to make an appointment for her *mutter*. Maybe Jessica hadn't told Dr. Kathleen about it. *Ne*. Jessica had said the doctor would look at *Vater* while she was here checking out *Mutter*.

Dr. Kathleen stood. "Thank you for the tea and cookies," she said to *Mutter*, then turned to *Vater*. "Though your shoulder is better, I don't want you using those crutches much yet. It still needs to heal, and I don't want you to reinjure it. Next week, I'll come back and start you on some exercises to strengthen it." Dr. Kathleen picked up her backpack of medical supplies and headed for the door. "Deborah, would you walk me out?"

Deborah rushed to her side and held the door open. "Of course." She followed her out, down the steps and across the yard to where Amos had parked the horse and buggy. Because this wasn't expected to be a long visit, the horse hadn't been unhitched.

Kathleen stopped next to her buggy. "Bring your *mutter* to my clinic tomorrow afternoon. I'll make sure I don't have any other appointments."

"You want to see her?"

Had she noticed? Or was the doctor simply granting Deborah the appointment she'd asked for?

"I didn't really see or hear anything out of the ordinary—except calling your sister by the wrong name—but there's something that seems off that I can't put my finger on. Add that with your concern, and it makes me want to see her in my clinic."

"I'll bring her. *Danki* for not saying anything about my calling about her."

"No one else knows?"

"Knows there's something wrong with *Mutter*? I think my *vater* and older sisters do, but no one will talk to me about it. I tried, but they brushed it aside or changed the subject. Do they know I called for an appointment? *Ne.* I think they would try to stop me. They seem to be ignoring the issues."

"People don't like to think that a loved one has problems. Especially in Amish communities. We think we should be able to pray *all* our problems away, but *Gott* never said we would be free of troubles. Look at the Apostles. They all had more troubles after Christ was crucified than before. I don't believe it's whether or not we have troubles that tests and shows our faith, but how we deal with them that can glorify *Gott*. Bring your *mutter*, and we'll see what's going on." Dr. Kathleen climbed into her buggy and drove away.

Deborah stared after her. So, the doctor *had* come to check on *Mutter* as well as *Vater*. Her relief was palpable.

From inside the barn, Amos watched Deborah, who was standing in the yard. The doctor had left, but she didn't retreat into the house or look as though she was going to move anytime soon. What was she doing? This could be a *gut* opportunity to talk with her.

He exited the barn and his heart rate increased the closer he got to where she still stood. "Is everything all right?"

She jerked around to face him. "What? What do you mean by that?"

"Your *vater*? I assume that's why the doctor stopped by."

"Oh, *ja*, *Vater*, he's doing well, Dr. Kathleen doesn't want him to use his arm much yet, she's going to start him on some exercises next week. That's all. Nothing more."

"Gut." He squinted a little. Why was she talking so fast? "Is something wrong?"

"Wrong? Why would you ask that?"

"You're frowning, asked why I asked and you're talking faster than normal."

"Talking fast? That's just because I'm cold." She rubbed her upper arms as though to prove her point.

Did she have another secret? "Maybe you should go back into the house." But he didn't want her to. He could fetch his coat for her to get her to stay.

"Oh, yeah. I should do that." She turned and walked away.

He wished he could call her back, but he didn't have a reason to do so.

She paused at the bottom of the steps to the front porch. Instead of going inside, she headed out across the field. Without her coat.

Going for a walk? Certainly she wouldn't head into Goshen to visit her friend this late in the afternoon. It would get dark before she could return.

He ran back inside the barn and grabbed his own coat, then trotted after her.

He caught up to her by the pond and sat on the log next to her. "I thought you might be going to visit your friend."

She scrunched up her face. "What? What friend?"

"The one in need you go to all the time."

Her eyes widened. "Oh. *That* friend. *Ne.* I just came out here to think. Did you come to check up on me?"

He held out his coat, which was still in his hand. "I thought you might get cold. You said you were cold before coming."

"*Danki.* That was very thoughtful. Won't you get cold?"

"*Ne.*" He wrapped it around her shoulders. "Do you want to be alone? I can leave."

"*Ne*, please stay." She shifted to face him better. "May I ask you a question?"

"Of course." He settled himself on the log.

"What if there was something you felt you should do—felt it was the *right* thing to do—but you knew your parents wouldn't approve if you asked them?"

Like leaving the Amish community? Her words could be describing his own dilemma. "If it truly is the right thing, wouldn't your parents tell you to do it?"

"Not if *they* thought it was wrong."

"Then how could it be right?"

"Sometimes, one person can view something as right and another view it as wrong."

Exactly. Like him leaving his Amish community to figure out where he belonged.

She continued, "So, what if there's a hungry child. The right thing to do is to give the child food, but the only food belongs to someone else. Is it wrong to take what belongs to someone else to feed the child? It wouldn't be right to let the child go hungry. No Amish person would deny a child food. So, it's like you have permission in advance."

Did her "friend in need" require food?

"That's a bad example." She waved her hand in the air. "Just forget it."

"*Ne.* I understand what you're trying to say. Do you truly want to know what I think?"

"*Ja.*"

"I think you need to decide if doing the right thing is…not more important, but more *right* than the wrong thing is wrong. If that makes sense."

"So, the right thing needs to be more right than it is wrong?"

"Something like that." Some of the church leaders wouldn't say so. Something was either right or wrong, it couldn't be a little of both. But some things weren't as clear.

"*Danki.* That's helpful."

He was glad he could help. Now he just needed to figure out for himself if his right thing was more right than the wrong part of it was wrong.

At this moment, sitting with Deborah seemed very right, but this moment couldn't last. Bartholomew would heal and not need help, and Amos would be expected to return to his parents' farm, which his brothers would split, leaving Amos to fend for himself. He wasn't a very *gut* Amish if he thought only of himself. He glanced over at Deborah. She deserved a better Amish man than he was turning out to be.

Chapter Ten

Deborah escorted her *mutter* into the barn. She glanced around for Amos but didn't see him. She was both grateful and disappointed. "Could you sit right there on that barrel until I get Floyd hitched up?" She didn't want her *mutter* wandering off.

Mutter complied. She seemed to be in a bit of a confused state but amenable.

Deborah retrieved the buggy harness from the wall outside the tack room. Though she tried to see Amos whenever she came out to the barn, it was *gut* he wasn't here right now. She wouldn't have to explain where she was going or what she was doing or why.

All the leather and metal in the harness weighed heavy in her arms. She hung the various parts on the pegs designed to hold the harness in preparation for putting it on the horse.

Then she walked Floyd out of his stall and tied his lead rope to a post. One of the kittens lay undisturbed upon the horse's back, and another stood on his withers and mane.

Amos's voice came from behind her. "Let me help with that."

She spun around, spooking the horse, who double-stepped in place.

Amos rushed over, reached around her with one arm and took hold of the rope. His other arm, which was on the other side of her, stroked the horse's neck. "Whoa, boy."

The horse settled with a snort.

Deborah's breath caught at him being so close.

Amos stared at Deborah for a moment, then cleared his throat. "I obviously startled you. You weren't expecting me to come in here—the place I spend the most time." He squinted mischievously. "Which makes me wonder what you're up to."

From his crooked grin, she knew he was teasing her. He liked to joke about where she went during the day and various other things. She would like nothing better than to stand there and look at him, but she didn't have time for his shenanigans today. "I'm not up to anything." She couldn't allow her serious mission to be thwarted.

He looked from her to her *mutter* and back. "You are up to something. You're taking her to see the doctor, aren't you?"

The temptation to lie tickled her tongue, but that would be wrong. She ducked under his arm instead. *"Ja."*

"Alone?"

She set a step stool next to Floyd's front legs. The horse was too tall for her to reach without it, even at five-nine. *"Ja."* Then she took the breast collar and climbed on the step.

Amos took hold of the collar, keeping her from putting it on the horse. "Does your *vater* know about this?"

She tried to pull the apparatus free. *Vater* couldn't

know until after Deborah found out what was wrong
with *Mutter.* "He ignores her condition. Even you noticed something was off with her."

He wrestled the collar from her hands. "You need
to tell your *vater.*"

"He'll say *ne.*" She stepped down from the stool.

"He's the head of your family. It's *his* decision."

Mutter appeared beside them. "Amos, introduce me
to your young lady."

Deborah squinted at *Mutter.* How could her *mutter*
not recognize her? Deborah's heart sank. She knew
Mutter rarely noticed when she was gone, but to not
even recognize her caused her heart to physically hurt.
Lately, *Mutter* had been getting worse. "*Mutter!* I'm
Deborah. Your daughter."

Mutter squinted and studied her middlemost daughter. Then recognition broke on her face. "Deborah!"

Pushing the stool aside with his foot, Amos wrapped
the collar around the horse's neck, causing the kitten on
Floyd's withers to jump off and scamper away.

"Now you're helping me?" She picked up the kitten
still lying on the draft horse's back and sent him off
with his sibling.

"I think your *vater* should know." Amos made short
work of harnessing Floyd and attaching the buggy. "But
if he isn't willing to get her the help she needs—" he
glanced at her *mutter,* who appeared to not realize she
was being talked about "—I think just this once, it will
be all right. See what the doctor has to say. As long as
no decisions are made without his consent."

Mutter jerked away from Deborah. "*Ne!* I'm not
going to a doctor. Doctors are bad. They hurt people."

Had it just now registered to her *mutter* that they

were going to the doctor's? "*Mutter*, you need to. The doctor's not going to hurt you. She's going to help you."

Mutter shook her head.

Hannah entered the barn.

Uh-oh. What would her sister do? This was getting more and more complicated by the minute. Could Deborah talk her sister in to leaving them be and allowing Deborah to take their *mutter*?

But before Deborah could do or say anything, *Mutter* rushed to Hannah's side. "Hannah won't let you."

Hannah took *Mutter's* hand in one of hers and patted it with the other. "*Ne, Mutter.* You misunderstood. You remember the Yoders."

"*Ja.*"

What was her sister doing?

"You remember Kathleen Yoder."

"*Ja.* She was such a sweet girl, but she left and never came back. We still pray for her."

"She *did* come back. Last year."

Mutter's eyes widened. "She did?"

"*Ja.* She's invited us for tea. You would like to visit with Kathleen, wouldn't you?"

"*Ja.*" The fear melted from *Mutter's* expression, and she climbed into the buggy without another word of protest. Hannah followed, settling herself in the back beside *Mutter*.

Deborah peered in the back. "You're coming with us?"

"You obviously need someone who knows how to handle *Mutter*."

She couldn't believe her sister was helping after brushing Deborah's concerns aside. She climbed in front.

Amos led the horse out of the barn, then fed the reins

through the rein slits at the bottom of the windshield. He climbed in.

Deborah cocked her head. "You're coming, too?"

He nodded and then set Floyd into motion.

She was grateful to have her sister and Amos along for support, as well as to help her make the best decision possible for *Mutter*.

Deborah's feelings tangled together. How could her *mutter* not remember her own daughter when she could recall two people outside of the family? One from fourteen years ago and the other she'd only known for two months.

Amos kept his voice low. "As soon as we return, you are going to tell your *vater* that we took her to the…to visit Kathleen and what she had to say."

Deborah nodded and kept her voice low as well. "If my *vater* knows that my *mutter* has a problem, why hasn't he done anything about it?"

"He's probably afraid."

She couldn't imagine. "My *vater* has never been afraid of anything."

"This is his *frau*. No one wants to think something is wrong with a family member."

"Ignoring it won't make it go away or make her suddenly better. I think she's getting worse."

From the back seat, Hannah said, "She is."

Deborah turned to face her sister. "What caused your change of heart? When she was out wandering, you acted like nothing was wrong. Now you're helping me?"

Mutter stared out the window with a contented smile on her face.

Hannah continued. "As you realized, *Mutter's* getting worse. She'd been quite manageable for years."

"She's been like this for years?" Deborah couldn't believe it. How had she not seen it?

"Not like she is now. Just the occasional lapse. Certain words and places set her off."

"Words like *doc*—"

"Don't. Let's not upset her needlessly. *Ja.* Words like that. Since *Vater's* accident she's gotten worse, and I never know what will set her off. As I said, she was manageable. I had hopes to marry Nehemiah Zook this fall, but I can't if *Mutter* is like this. She needs constant supervision lately."

Deborah had had no idea what her sisters had been dealing with all these years. "When did you first notice something about her?"

"When Lydia and I were ten or so, *Vater* told us to keep an eye on her. She had disappeared a couple of times, and *Vater* had to go find her. He told us she'd just taken a walk and gone farther than she meant to."

"I like taking walks," *Mutter* said, still gazing out the window.

Was that where Deborah got her affinity for taking walks? Was she going to end up like her?

Hannah continued, "By the time we were twelve, we knew something wasn't right."

"So if Lydia knows about *Mutter*, why didn't she come, too?"

"She's going to keep *Vater* occupied so he doesn't question where *Mutter* has gone and keep Naomi and Sarah under control."

Her oldest sisters were helping her. "What about Miriam? Does she know?"

"*Ja.* She's afraid of never marrying, as well."

"Is that why she's never agreed to have a boy court her?" So, it was just as well that Amos wasn't interested in her.

Hannah nodded. "None of us see how we can. *Vater* can't run the farm and keep an eye on *Mutter.*"

Was *Mutter* really that bad off that her daughters felt as though they could never marry? Because of *Mutter's* condition, she probably hadn't noticed when any of her daughters went missing, let alone Deborah. With her older sisters busy keeping an eye on *Mutter*, they either didn't notice Deborah's frequent absences, or they just didn't have the energy to keep track of their *mutter* and watch over an eight-year-old Down syndrome sister *and* a sister who could take care of herself. Not to mention Naomi's neediness.

This was a lot to digest. She would let it all sit and simmer until after the visit to the doctor. She didn't want to think about it all right now, so she turned her thoughts to more pleasant things. Like the handsome man seated next to her—a man who was both kind and helpful. Gratitude filled her at his presence.

When Amos pulled the buggy to a stop in front of the clinic, Hannah said in a light friendly voice, "Deborah, go tell *Kathleen* we're here for *tea* and a *visit.*"

Deborah understood to forewarn the doctor about the state of their *mutter.* She got out of the buggy and hurried inside. Jessica Yoder, the doctor's sister and receptionist, sat at a desk just inside the door. Deborah stopped short. Jessica smiled and greeted her warmly. "*Hallo.* Dr. Kathleen is expecting you. We thought you were bringing your *mutter.*"

"She's coming right behind me. I need to—"

Dr. Kathleen came out of her office. "You made it. Is your *mutter* with you?"

"Right behind me. She thinks we're here for tea and a visit. She became very upset when she learned we were coming to see a doctor."

Dr. Kathleen smiled. "Then today I'm simply Kathleen." She gave her sister a pointed look. Her sister nodded back in understanding. "And we shall have a nice visit."

Jessica jumped to her feet. "I'll get the tea started. We have half of a cake. I'll slice it."

Amos opened the door for Hannah and *Mutter.* Then he came in and closed it behind them.

Dr. Kathleen greeted *Mutter* and had her sit on the sofa in the waiting room, which used to be a living room and still resembled one. At least well enough that *Mutter* wouldn't notice the difference. Hannah sat next to her.

Dr. Kathleen looked at Amos. "Normally, only family members are present at something like this."

Hannah spoke up. "He knows. It's fine if he stays."

"Very well, then." Dr. Kathleen sat in a chair nearest to *Mutter.*

Jessica brought them each a slice of cake and a cup of tea.

Deborah sat in a chair across from the sofa, next to Jessica.

Amos separated himself from the group of women and sat in the chair behind the small desk that Jessica had occupied. He looked like a man at a quilting party. He fidgeted as though uncomfortable, but he stayed. He could have excused himself and kept occupied outside, or even gone to find Noah Lambright, Dr. Kathleen's husband, but Amos chose to stay. That said a lot about him.

But just what did it say about him? Did it say he was interested in what was wrong with her *mutter*? Did it say he cared? Or did it just say that he was nosy? Whatever the reason, his being here calmed Deborah. When it came time to talk to her *vater* about all this and tell him that she, Hannah, Lydia and Amos had gone behind his back to take her *mutter* to see a doctor, Amos could be an advocate on their side. Maybe her *vater* would be more likely to listen to another man.

Amos studied Deborah as the women talked. He wasn't sure staying was the best choice. He just knew he wanted to be here for Deborah. If she needed him. If her *mutter* forgot who she was again. How terrible for her own *mutter* to not recognize her. He couldn't imagine.

Dr. Kathleen skillfully questioned Teresa Miller, not once letting the older woman know that she was being examined. She asked questions about her daughters and husband, about the farm, about when she was married. He couldn't tell how the answers gave anything away that might be wrong. She seemed perfectly normal, but he knew she wasn't.

When Deborah glanced his way, which seemed to be often, he gave her a smile. Most of the time she returned his offer of encouragement in kind.

Dr. Kathleen leaned forward. "Teresa, would you help Jessica in the kitchen make a fresh pot of tea?"

Jessica rose.

When Teresa stood and had her back to the doctor, Kathleen mouthed to her sister, *Keep her in there.* She took a pad of paper from the end table next to her.

Jessica nodded. The two crossed the large room and went through the open doorway into the kitchen.

Amos moved from his place at the desk and sat in the chair Jessica had vacated, right next to Deborah. Though he liked sitting near to her, it was harder to watch her from this vantage point.

Dr. Kathleen spoke in a soft voice. "Tell me what you've noticed that concerns you."

"Hannah, you've known about her condition the longest, maybe you should start," Deborah said.

Dr. Kathleen looked at Hannah. "That sounds like a *gut* idea." Then she glanced at Deborah and Amos in turn. "But I want to hear from each of you. One person may notice something the others don't."

Hannah cleared her throat. "*Mutter* has always been a little different from the other *mutters*, but nothing concerning. I guess I was eight or so when I realized other *mutters* weren't the same as mine. Lydia and I would whisper about it in bed at night. When we were ten, *Vater* asked us to keep an eye on *Mutter*. We didn't understand why, but we did as we were told. Each night, *Vater* would ask us what *Mutter* did that day. He would ask specific questions, like if she ever just stood and stared. We thought it was some sort of game."

No wonder one of the twins always gave him directions instead of their *mutter* when their *vater* wasn't around. They were shielding Teresa and making sure no one knew she had a problem.

Kathleen wrote on her paper. "What were the repeated things you told him?"

"She would stare off into space like she saw something interesting someplace else. She would call my twin and me by each other's names, which we thought was fun. For a long time, we thought we were *gut* at fooling her. Now we feel bad for doing it. She would wander off and not know where she was."

"What were the most unusual things she did?"

"She put the bowl of cake batter in the oven, and the oven wasn't even on. She hung the dirty clothes on the clothesline. She would forget one of us was her daughter. She would cry for no reason."

Kathleen turned to Amos. "You've been at the Miller farm for only a short time. Have you noticed anything?"

He shifted in his chair. It felt wrong to talk about her this way. He turned toward Deborah, and she nodded for him to go ahead. Knowing she was all right with him talking about her *mutter* made him feel better about this. If it would ultimately help Teresa, he needed to report his observations. "She recognized me before Deborah. When we were hitching up the horse to come here, she asked me to introduce her to my young lady." Remembering the hurt look on Deborah's face made his chest ache all over again. "She forgets things. I found her wandering in the road. She didn't know why she was out there. She's called me by other people's names. I thought it was because I was new on the farm and she couldn't remember my name."

Kathleen asked Deborah, "Does your *mutter* often forget who you are?"

"*Ja.*"

"More so than your sisters?"

"I used to think I was the *only* one she forgot, but now I wonder if everyone isn't forgotten." Deborah stared at her oldest sister.

A sheepish expression crossed Hannah's face. "She seems to forget Deborah more than anyone else. She's gotten worse since our *vater* broke his leg. Instead of the occasional slipup, it's happening most days. We used to be able to manage her so others wouldn't notice. It's become more and more difficult."

Kathleen wrote some more. "I remember when your *vater* got hurt. She was quite upset. I thought it was just because she feared losing him. I gave her something to calm her on the ride to the hospital, but now I'm afraid that just masked her condition."

Hannah nodded. "I wondered why she seemed calmer at the hospital and around doctors than we expected her to be."

"Has she had any serious accidents with head trauma?"

"Not that I can remember," Hannah said.

"Has she had any serious illnesses with a high fever?"

"I don't know," Hannah answered again.

Kathleen nodded. "I'm going to need access to her medical records." She excused herself for a moment. When she returned, she held out a piece of paper. "This form needs to be filled out and signed."

Hannah took the form. "I can do that."

Dr. Kathleen shook her head. "You can fill it out, but we need either your *mutter's* signature or your *vater's* on her behalf."

Hannah stared at the form. "I'll fill it out, and then I'll have our *mutter* sign it."

Kathleen glanced at their *mutter's* back through the kitchen doorway, then returned her gaze to Hannah. "She needs to understand what she's signing, or I can't submit it in good conscience."

Hannah nodded. "I can make her understand well enough."

"I would prefer your *vater* be apprised of this. He should give his consent, as well."

"Does he have to?" Hannah said.

"Legally? *Ne.* But because your *mutter* is Amish and her husband is head of the household, he should be involved, or we could all be shunned for going behind his back."

Deborah and Hannah nodded.

Amos broke his silence. "Do you suspect that Teresa

might have fallen and hit her head or had some illness that caused her problems?"

"Those are two possibilities. If she has had either, it will give us a direction to look in. If not, that, too, will give us other avenues to search."

Amos hesitated but felt the subject no one seemed to want to bring up needed to be. "You haven't mentioned it, but could she have Alzheimer's disease?"

"Let's not use that label yet. It could be any number of things. I need to order more tests before I go there."

Deborah spoke up. "What if we can't get our *vater's* permission? What do we do then? Leave our *mutter* like this?"

"Let's see what he says first. I'm sure he wants what's best for her."

What the doctor thought was best might not be the same as what Bartholomew Miller thought.

Deborah had a pinched expression and looked like she might cry.

He wanted to wrap his arms around her and comfort her. Not only would that be inappropriate, but he also didn't know how to do it without others seeing.

But since he couldn't do that, maybe he could find a way to convince Bartholomew that there was no shame in seeking counsel from the doctor.

Chapter Eleven

After the visit to the doctor's, Deborah sat on the porch with her *vater*. She and her sisters agreed she might have the best chance to convince him to release *Mutter's* medical records and get her diagnosed. She could give a fresh perspective. The twins had been *Vater's* confidantes and helpers for years. Maybe he would listen to someone else, but she wished Amos was beside her for moral support. "*Vater*? May I talk to you?" Her twin sisters were right inside, listening, ready to step forward if necessary.

"Of course. Any of you girls can always come to me. I think I know what this is about."

"You do?"

But he didn't seem upset. Instead, he looked almost happy. "Amos?"

"Amos?" Just the mention of his name made something happy swirl around inside her despite the current circumstances. "*Ne.* Why would you say that?" Did her *vater* know she had feelings for him? How embarrassing.

"I see the way you look at him, and the way he looks at you."

Amos looked at her in a certain way? The same way

she tried *not* to look at him? She mentally shook her head. Before the conversation had even started, *Vater* had derailed her. "I don't want to talk about Amos." Not that she didn't enjoy talking about him, but now wasn't the time. She tamped down her feelings for the kind farmhand. "I want to talk about *Mutter.*"

Vater's congenial attitude fell away as he stood and tucked his crutches under his arms. "*Mutter* is well." He hobbled down the steps and across the yard.

He obviously didn't want to talk about the painful subject. He'd shut her down before she'd even started. Should she go after him?

The front door opened. Hannah, Lydia and Miriam stepped out onto the porch.

Deborah faced them. "I'll go after him and try again."

Miriam heaved a sigh as though defeated.

Lydia shook her head. "*Vater* doesn't want to hear about *Mutter.*" She sounded defeated, as well.

Hannah planted her hands on her hips. "Well, he's going to. He can't ignore this any longer. Come on. We'll *all* talk to him. He can't ignore four of us at once." Hannah headed toward the barn, where *Vater* had gone, with Lydia and Miriam on her heels.

Deborah trailed after her three older sisters. Amos had said it wasn't a *gut* idea to have them all gang up on *Vater* at once. "But what about *Mutter*, Naomi and Sarah?"

"I told Joanna to keep them all in the house." Hannah strode with determination in her steps.

How much did seventeen-year-old Joanna know? She knew enough to obey Hannah.

Deborah stood shoulder-to-shoulder with her sisters as they entered the barn, having automatically lined up from oldest to youngest. They would be able to speak freely with him out here, where neither the younger girls nor *Mutter* would hear.

Though they'd told Amos that they would deal with their *vater* themselves, he was in the barn as normal. Hannah and Lydia didn't want him involved because *Vater* had tried to keep this within the family and didn't want to embarrass him by bringing in an outsider. Maybe that was why *Vater* had come out here, to keep them from broaching a subject he didn't want to talk about.

Deborah had wanted Amos in on the discussion. He'd been a big help in taking *Mutter* to see the doctor, and she treasured his support.

Hannah drew in a deep breath. "*Vater*, we need to talk about *Mutter*."

He shook his head. "Is this why you girls followed me out here?" He glanced toward Amos, who stood in the doorway of the cow's stall. "This is not the place."

Amos leaned the mucking shovel against the wall and strode past them all. "I'll be outside if anyone needs me." He gave Deborah a pointed look and a nod.

Her insides danced, and she nodded back out of appreciation, both because he was giving the family privacy, and because he would be available should they need him. What she wanted to do was hold on to him to stop her world from tipping out of control, and right now, he felt like the only solid thing in her life, but she let him leave without a word.

Hannah took a step forward. "*Vater*, Lydia and I want to get married, but we can't leave *Mutter* without someone to look after her. I think Miriam has settled on never marrying, because she thinks she can't. She'll take on the responsibility of *Mutter* and become an old maid, but I know she would like to marry and have a family of her own. We hate to saddle her with this job. We need to do something about *Mutter*."

Vater glared at his eldest, then shifted his gaze to Deborah. "Deborah, go in the house."

Deborah wasn't sure what to do. Obey her *vater*? Or stay put? She was the one who had taken their *mutter* to Dr. Kathleen.

Miriam gripped Deborah's wrist and said in a quiet voice, "Stay."

Lydia spoke up. "*Vater*, Deborah knows all about *Mutter's*…issues."

His gaze darted from daughter to daughter to daughter. "She doesn't know. She doesn't understand."

Hannah spoke up this time. "She does know. Deborah and I took *Mutter* to see Dr. Kathleen."

"You did what? You told the doctor? Behind my back? This is a private family matter."

Lydia, the peacemaker, took *Vater* by the arm. "We all know that *Mutter* needs special help and guidance. If we deny that, we can't help her. We want to do what's best for her."

Hannah added, "And for the whole family."

Deborah shifted her feet. "And for you, too."

Vater glared at each of his daughters in turn. Then the fight went out of his eyes, and he seemed as though he was giving in, just a little bit. "Your *mutter* is just fine. We've always been able to take care of her."

"*Ne*, she's not fine." Deborah didn't know where that burst of courage had come from, but for some strange reason, she sensed it might be that Amos was nearby.

"Things can't continue this way," Hannah said. "We can only take care of her if none of us ever marries or leaves."

Lydia jumped back in. "*Mutter* is getting worse."

"*Ne*, she's not. I won't listen to any more of this nonsense." *Vater* glanced toward the barn opening. "This isn't the place to discuss this."

Hannah squared her shoulders. "This is precisely the place. Amos went with us to see the doctor."

Vater's eyes widened. "You told him our family's problems?"

Deborah took a step forward. "We didn't have to. He's seen *Mutter's* odd behavior and figured it out." Amos knowing and being understanding about it strengthened her resolve. None of them could excuse this away now that an outsider knew.

Vater clenched his jaw and hobbled around in a circle. He looked as though he'd wanted to storm away again, but his crutches made that difficult. He stopped and faced the open doorway. "Amos! Come back in here!" He had spoken loud enough for someone to hear if they'd been right outside but didn't quite yell. He obviously thought Amos stood close by, listening.

Amos didn't appear.

Vater huffed out a breath. "Deborah, go get the boy. I'll see what he has to say for himself."

Deborah froze in place. Would *Vater* scold Amos? Send him away from the farm?

Hannah stepped forward. "*Vater*, he's done nothing wrong."

"This is my *frau* we are talking about. My family. I will speak to him if I wish." He turned back to Deborah. "Get the boy."

Amos was hardly a boy, but Deborah backed out of the barn. Had *Vater* sent her away to once again exclude her from a conversation with her older sisters? She would ask them later. She refused to be shut out again.

Amos stood by the woodpile, swinging the ax. Definitely *not* a boy. He hadn't been listening. She thought more highly of him for that and wanted to run into his arms.

The tool came down on a log, and the two halves toppled in opposite directions. He leaned to pick up the larger one.

"Amos?"

With the log in hand, he turned and smiled. *"Ja?"*

Her mouth momentarily responded in kind, then she remembered why she'd been sent out here. "My *vater* wishes you to come back in. We told him you know about our *mutter*. He isn't happy."

He tossed the hunk of wood on the ground with several others. "I'm sure he isn't. All of this can't be easy for him."

Her sisters hadn't wanted Amos involved for *Vater's* sake, but Deborah believed he could help. Show *Vater* that people outside the family could be kind to *Mutter*, as well. *Vater* might not have wanted Amos to know, but he already did. Deborah wanted him at her side to draw from his strength. She walked with him back inside the barn.

Her sisters and *Vater* stood in silence.

Amos approached slowly.

Vater became stiff and set his jaw. "Girls, leave us."

Oh, dear. Deborah hoped *Vater* didn't blame Amos and reprimand him. She wanted to stay at his side to lend support. "*Vater*, I don't think we can keep this a secret from the community any longer. I'm sure some people already suspect something is wrong with *Mutter*. The way Hannah or Lydia are always close beside her and shield her from others. How they talk for her."

Vater took a slow breath. "Go inside the house and wait for me there. Let us men talk."

Deborah glanced from *Vater* to Amos. Amos nodded that he would be fine and gave her a reassuring smile that calmed her inside.

With reluctance, she and her sisters moved toward the door. Defying *Vater* wouldn't help Amos.

She sent up a quick prayer for Amos.

Amos faced Bartholomew Miller, bracing himself for the man's ire. He had volunteered to speak to Bartholomew, but now he wasn't so sure of the wisdom in that. This was a family matter. Amos wasn't family. Bartholomew would likely send him away from the farm entirely. If that was the case, he would take his belongings and text Jacob to come get him. He would sleep in the back of his cousin's pickup if he had to.

The older man shifted on his crutches. His expression was weary and haggard. The poor man looked worn-out. Not only had he been saddled with all daughters—not one son to help shoulder the workload of a farm—but he also had a child with Down syndrome and a *frau* with medical problems. So many burdens for one man to bear.

Amos wished Bartholomew would sit down but knew he likely wouldn't. That would be a sign of weakness. "I want to help you, your *frau* and your family in any way I can." He'd grown to care a great deal about this family. In fact, he felt more comfortable with them than his own. He had a useful place here, unlike on his *vater's* farm.

Bartholomew nodded. "Anything we say here needs to stay between the two of us."

"I understand."

"We'll talk man-to-man. Women can be too emotional. Tell me what you've noticed about my *frau*."

Unusual for an Amish man to talk to another about so personal a subject. Maybe to the bishop or one of the elders, but not a young man such as himself. He hoped the older man didn't think him disrespectful. After all, what kind of counsel could a young, single man give a married one old enough to be his father? But the unique position Amos found himself in—working on their farm for weeks and living in the barn—gave him an advantage others in the community didn't have. He would adhere to Bartholomew's wishes and not speak to anyone about this, and he would proceed with the utmost respect. "I can tell your *frau* loves all of you a lot."

"But?"

"But…" Speaking of this made him uncomfortable. He wished he could just listen, but silence wouldn't help Teresa Miller or her family. "She forgets things and gets confused. When we were hitching up the buggy to take her to the doctor's, she asked me to introduce the girl with me. It was Deborah. Her own daughter. She remembered me but not her." Poor Deborah. The ache for her welled anew. He couldn't imagine his own *mutter* forgetting him. "She forgets other things, too, and wanders sometimes like she doesn't know where she is. Your daughters do a *gut* job of shielding her, but they can't always. I found her on the road a week after I arrived here. I didn't think much of it, but now I know better. What if she wanders off and gets hurt or lost?"

Bartholomew stared at Amos for a long minute before he spoke. "I appreciate your candor and compassion for my *frau* and daughters." He paused. "What would you do if you were me?"

Gott, guard my words and help me say the right things. Was Amos prepared to give an older man advice about his *frau*? "I think…I would try to figure out what's causing her to forget and be confused. Dr. Kathleen needs her medical history and records to diagnose her properly. She requires your permission. Maybe there's a treatment that can help your *frau* remember."

"And if there's not?"

So he feared there would be no help or hope for his *frau*.

"Then I guess we'll deal with it at that point. We can't help her properly until we know what's wrong."

"We?"

"*Ja.* The more people who can look out for her, the safer she'll be."

"You aren't suggesting I tell the rest of the community, are you?"

"Wouldn't that be better than keeping secrets and something bad happening to her?"

Bartholomew backed up and sat on an upturned log that served as a stool. "I do want her to be safe."

"I can tell. That's why you've had your daughters keeping such a close watch on her for so long. It can't hurt to speak to Dr. Kathleen. She's compassionate and discreet."

"I wish to say *ne*, but you—" he waved a crutch in the general direction of the house "—and my daughters make sense. I can't ignore the Lord's prodding any longer. I don't want any of my daughters to remain single when they want to marry. I just wanted to keep Teresa close and protect her."

"I think the best way to protect her is to let others— not a lot of people, but a few who can help—know what's going on with her."

"I do want to protect her. Take me to the doctor's."

This conversation went better and easier than Amos

imagined. The older man must have been ready. "Right now?"

"*Ja*, right now. I shouldn't wait." Bartholomew had been ready for this step. He'd just needed a little nudge.

"Do you want me to tell your daughters where we're going and what you're doing?"

Bartholomew heaved a sigh. "They'll want to come with us. I'll go inside and tell them and call the doctor to let her know we're coming."

Amos figured at least one of his daughters would want to come, if not several of them. Would that be such a bad thing? He set to work on hitching the larger buggy while Bartholomew crutched inside.

Soon, Amos had the buggy ready and parked in front of the house.

Bartholomew, Deborah, Hannah and Lydia came out onto the porch. *Ah*. Deborah was coming. *Gut*.

The girls climbed into the back. Before Amos could help Bartholomew into the front, the door opened again, and Teresa came out. "I'm not ready yet. Let me get my coat."

Bartholomew took his *frau's* arm and spoke gently to her. "I need you to stay here with the younger children."

Teresa's eyebrows scrunched down. "Stay? But…I…"

Miriam joined them on the porch. "*Mutter*, I need your help hemming my dress."

Teresa's eyes brightened. "*Ja*, I can help you." She turned back to her husband. "I'm needed here, so I won't be able to go with you."

Bartholomew smiled at his daughter, then at his *frau*. "That's all right. Maybe next time."

The pair of women went back inside, and Amos helped Bartholomew maneuver his casted leg and his crutches into the buggy.

Tension filled the buggy during the slow ride.

Finally, they arrived at the doctor's. It sure was nice to have one right in their community, and that she was one of their own, who understood so much more than an outsider could. Amos helped everyone out, and Noah Lambright, the doctor's husband, took over the care of the horse and buggy so Amos could go inside the *dawdy haus* clinic with the others.

With no other patients there, Dr. Kathleen offered them seats in the waiting room to accommodate their large group, which was too big to fit in the exam room comfortably. Since her sister had gone for the day, the doctor brought them each a cup of tea or coffee. "How are you doing, Bartholomew? Are you having any trouble with your shoulder or getting around on your crutches?"

"*Ne.* I'm doing well."

"Are the physical-therapy exercises helping?"

"*Ja.* We didn't come for me."

Dr. Kathleen nodded. "Teresa?"

Bartholomew took a slow breath. "*Ja.* She's not doing well, as my daughters have already told you."

"I saw for myself. I'd like to do some tests, but I need your permission and to have access to her medical records."

"You have my permission."

"I'll need it in writing." Dr. Kathleen brought out the required documents, filled in the needed information and had Bartholomew sign them. "Now, tell me a bit about your *frau's* medical history. When did you first notice something wasn't quite right with her?"

"When she was carrying Hannah and Lydia. I thought it was just part of being pregnant. But she continued after they were born for a few months and slowly returned to her normal self. She got worse with each successive pregnancy."

"Has she had any operations?"

"She had one tonsil removed when she was six and again when she was ten, and her appendix out six months later."

Dr. Kathleen made notes. "Any accidents?"

"She was in a buggy accident when she was three. Two of her siblings and her *mutter* didn't survive, and she was in the hospital for a couple of weeks. She had a dizzy spell and fell while she was carrying Deborah, and when Deborah was born, Teresa lost a lot of blood."

Amos couldn't imagine all that happening to one person.

No wonder she forgot Deborah most. She'd had quite a bit of trauma with her. Amos glanced at Deborah. Her eyes glistened. Was she about to cry? He wanted to wipe away her tears.

Bartholomew chuckled. "Not surprising that she doesn't like doctors. She's never had *gut* experiences with them."

Dr. Kathleen smiled. "I noticed. I hope to be as much her friend as her doctor. Childhood diseases?"

"All the normal ones, chicken pox and the like."

Dr. Kathleen listed off a multitude of childhood diseases that Bartholomew answered affirmative to. "Chronic problems?"

"Like what? Being forgetful and confused?"

"Other things like a cough that won't go away, regular headaches, persistent rash?"

Bartholomew shook his head.

Hannah jumped in. "She does get quite a few headaches, and her hands shake."

Lydia nodded her agreement.

"Shake? How?"

"Her hands are usually at her sides, and they twitch, sort of." Hannah stood and demonstrated.

"And the headaches? Is there anything different going on when she gets those? Same time of day? Certain situations?"

Lydia answered this time, "When she's stressed, which happens after she's been confused. That's when her hands shake most, too."

This time, Hannah nodded.

Bartholomew stared at his twin daughters. "I had no idea."

Both gave him identical tight smiles, but Hannah spoke. "We handled it so you could take care of the farm."

Lydia spoke up. "But her episodes are getting more frequent."

"And lasting longer," Hannah added. "We need to keep a constant watch on her."

From the stunned looks, neither Bartholomew nor Deborah knew any of this last part. Deborah swiped a tear from her cheek. Amos wished he could comfort her. Tell her everything would be all right.

After all the questions were answered, Dr. Kathleen made arrangements to go to their house to draw blood for tests.

Would Amos be invited to the *appointment*? What would the doctor ask all the others, and what would her diagnosis be? He would have to wait and see.

He glanced at Deborah. She held her jaw stiff as though she had something important caught between her teeth. He wished there was something he could do for her.

Deborah struggled to hold her tears at bay the whole ride home from their visit to Dr. Kathleen's. She had no idea her *mutter* had been through so much. Instead of going into the house with the others, she headed across the field to the pond. She plopped down on the fallen log and let the tears come.

How could she not have known what her own *mutter* was going through? She had been selfish and thinking of only herself while her *mutter* suffered. Running off whenever she could. Behaving like a spoiled child. Parading in front of a camera. Should she quit modeling? How could she continue and help look after her *mutter*?

"Deborah?"

She jumped at her name, stood and turned to face Amos, slapping away her tears. "I...um..."

"Are you all right?"

"Of course. Why wouldn't I be?" She didn't want him, of all people, to see her as an emotional mess.

"You heard some pretty upsetting things at the doctor's. I suspect you didn't know all that about your *mutter*."

Her emotions welled up and threatened to douse her in another wave of tears. Blinking several times, she swallowed hard. "I know now."

"Don't cry."

"I'm not crying."

He stepped forward and rubbed his thumb across her cheek. "Then what's this?" On his thumb sat a fledgling tear.

His touch sent a shiver through her.

"A raindrop?"

He looked up at the cloudless sky. "Okay. A raindrop."

His sweetness opened the floodgates, and she covered her face with her hands and sobbed.

Strong arms wrapped around her. "It's going to be all right. Your *mutter's* going to get the help she needs."

He shouldn't be holding her. Though not forbidden, it was frowned upon, but she didn't care. She needed the comfort. She needed the comfort from *him*. "I never knew she went through so much. I was too busy feeling sorry for myself to notice."

"It sounded like they all did a *gut* job of hiding her condition from you and everyone."

She pulled back but not out of his embrace. "I'm her *daughter*. I should have noticed."

"You did notice. You just interpreted the information inaccurately."

She considered that. She had noticed *Mutter's* forgetfulness and took it as a personal affront. She'd noticed her *mutter* acting out of touch and assumed that was where Deborah had gotten her flights of fancy. And she'd noticed *Mutter* wandering off and thought she just liked walks alone, as Deborah did.

She gritted her teeth to keep the tears at bay. No use. They came anyway. "I'm sorry. I'm a blubbering idiot."

"You're not an idiot. You're a caring daughter."

His kindness overwhelmed her.

Amos brushed away her tears again with his thumbs.

She shouldn't let him do that but reveled in his attention. It felt *gut* to have someone notice her and care about her. She gazed up into his sturdy brown eyes.

He gazed back.

Her insides wiggled. A pleasant yet scary feeling.

She should move.

But didn't.

She should look away.

But didn't.

She should…

"Deborah," he whispered, inches from her face.

His warm breath fanned her cheek.

"*Ja.*"

He leaned closer.

Then she heard her name again as though from a faraway dream, but Amos hadn't opened his mouth.

She heard it again, shrill this time.

Amos jerked away from her.

Deborah stepped back.

Naomi tromped toward them. "*Vater* wants you in the house."

Of course, Naomi would spoil the moment, but it was just as well. She had no right standing here with Amos. No right staring at him as though there was something between them.

Her sister maneuvered between them to walk next to Amos.

Deborah's moment of being noticed had been crushed once again by Naomi.

When she went inside the house, she found Hannah, Lydia and Miriam working in the kitchen. Joanna and Sarah's voices came from the living room, as well as *Mutter's* and *Vater's*.

Perfect, Amos and Naomi were still outside. Though Deborah would rather be with Amos, she would take this opportunity to speak to her three older sisters without anyone else around. "I'm glad you three are here."

"You are?" Miriam said. "Why us?"

Deborah kept her voice low. "Because you three seemed to know all about *Mutter's* problem. Why didn't any of you ever say anything or tell me? I could have helped."

Lydia opened her mouth but didn't say anything when Hannah held up her hand. Hannah, always in charge. "That was my decision, and I came to regret it. It was easier in the beginning for Lydia and me to handle *Mutter*. We worked well as a team and reported back to *Vater*. But when Sarah came along and was so needy and Naomi became jealous of all the time she demanded, it became harder to manage it all. Miriam partially figured things out and started pitching in and helping. So, we three worked together to manage *Mutter*, placate Naomi, deal with Sarah and take care of the house. You and Joanna always took care of yourselves, which was a huge help. We didn't have to worry about you."

"But if you had told me, I could have helped instead of just 'not being a bother.'"

"You're right. We should have."

Miriam finally spoke up. "Hannah and Lydia want to marry in the fall, so I'm going to take over everything they've been doing. I sure could use your help."

"What about you? Don't you want to get married?"

Miriam's words came out flat. "I'm praying the Lord won't have me fall in love." Her shoulders bowed forward.

Deborah had never heard of any woman in their community not *wanting* to get married.

Miriam's eyes watered. "That's a sacrifice I can make."

"*Ne*. You don't have to. Dr. Kathleen will figure out what's wrong with *Mutter* and make her better."

"And if she can't make *Mutter* better?" Lydia said.

Deborah didn't want to think that way, but she must consider it. "Teach me everything about taking care of her before you two marry. Then Miriam and I will teach Joanna."

Hannah spoke. "Then when Miriam marries and you marry and Joanna marries, do you honestly think Naomi will pick up the slack?"

Lydia's expression held both hope and defeat. "Let's wait and see what Dr. Kathleen says."

The strangest feeling engulfed Deborah. Like she actually belonged in her own family. Finally. She'd felt like a stranger for so long, she hadn't known *how* to belong. But now she knew *why* she'd felt like an outsider. She *had been* an outsider.

Her *vater* and her older sisters had been so caught up in surrounding *Mutter* to protect her that they hadn't realized they were cutting off the rest of the family. Deborah liked this new camaraderie with her sisters.

Now Deborah was in on the horrible secret.

Now she was included and would be there to help.

Now she wouldn't be left out.

She belonged.

Chapter Twelve

Deborah hated waiting. Yesterday, Dr. Kathleen and her sister, Jessica, arrived at the house just after breakfast and amazingly drew blood from everyone, including Amos, without a fuss from *Mutter* when it was her turn. True to her word, Dr. Kathleen had kept the visit friendly, like a neighbor dropping by.

Now they all had to wait for the results. Deborah couldn't pretend to be busy around the house but actually do nothing. She needed to get out. Get away. She was scheduled for a photo shoot today that she *had* planned to skip, but it offered the perfect distraction.

She peered out the kitchen window. Amos still puttered around the yard. Why did he have to pick today to work outside, cutting wood for the small potbellied stove in his little room? She'd interrupted this chore the other day. How much wood did he need? The room wasn't that big.

Before that he'd inspected the outside of the barn and repaired the chicken coop, which wasn't even broken. Granted, it did need help, but it wasn't quite broken yet. It just leaned slightly. And he ambled around doing other busywork in the yard. A lot of things needed some

TLC. Being the only man on the farm, *Vater* could never quite get to everything that needed attention.

If she didn't leave soon, she would be late and miss meeting her ride into town. Her sisters were easy to get away from, but Amos proved to be difficult. He kept a vigilant watch over the entire farm and its inhabitants.

She could tell him she was going to meet her "friend in need," but she didn't want to be questioned about that. She needed to devise a plan. If she went out the front door, he wouldn't be able to see her leave the house.

After slipping out, she went the long way around the house, away from where he worked. The chopping had ceased. Where was he now?

She peered around the house and directly into his broad chest.

"Where are you off to?" He smiled down at her. "Sneaking off?"

Why did he have to be so observant?

She forced a smile. "Just heading to the pond."

"*Wunderbar.* I'll go with you."

Ne! she wanted to say but held her tongue. If she protested, he might get suspicious. Hopefully, he would get bored quickly and want to return. She trudged slowly in the direction of the pond, hoping he would give up before they reached it.

He didn't.

She sat in her favorite spot on a log. The once fully frozen pond had half melted. Spring warmth was just around the corner. Some ducks walked on the frozen edge while others paddled around in the slushy center.

Amos sat on the log a couple of feet away from her. Even though she needed to be somewhere else, she liked having him here with her. Liked sharing her special spot, but as much as she wanted to, today was not the day to enjoy this. "I'm sure you have to get back to work."

"It can wait awhile. I can see why you like to come here a lot. It's nice. Peaceful."

And usually, she was all alone. The way she liked it. She stood. "I feel bad about keeping you. Let's head back."

He stood, as well. "I *should* get back. The corral needs some work."

She walked at a brisker pace than she'd walked out to the pond to get him off her tracks. Once he got busy with the corral, she would be able to hustle away.

While he was in the barn gathering tools, Deborah ran through the field, making sure to keep the barn between her and the corral to hide her escape. She tramped as quickly as possible through the bumpy field. She needed this shoot today. Needed to forget about her family's problems for a little while.

Out of breath, she reached her rendezvous spot, but the car wasn't there. She'd missed her ride. Now what was she going to do? Should she call Hudson from one of the Amish phone boxes near the road and tell him she couldn't make it today? Or start walking into town and be even later? She headed off along the road. She didn't want to go back home. Not after all the trouble she'd taken to escape.

After five minutes, a car drove past and pulled off to the side of the rode. The driver rolled down the window and waved for Deborah to come over.

She approached the vehicle and recognized the driver. "*Hallo*, Mrs. Carpenter." She had received rides from her before.

"Deborah, right?"

She nodded.

"Do you need a ride into town?"

"I would love a ride. I can pay for the gas."

"No need. I'm going that way anyway."

Deborah got in. "I was late for meeting my ride and missed it."

"Well, it's a good thing the Lord had me driving on this road today." Mrs. Carpenter dropped off Deborah at the gas station a couple of blocks from the photography studio.

Deborah never had anyone drop her off right at the studio. She didn't need to be questioned about what she was doing or telling other Amish exactly where she went. Amos wanted to know her whereabouts, but he was the last person she wanted to know, aside from the church leaders.

After all, she wasn't doing anything wrong. She never wore revealing clothes, and she wasn't hurting anyone.

Not really.

She had planned to model until she found a husband then quit. She figured she'd have a nice bit of money to help her husband buy a farm. In fact, she was doing a *gut* thing. But with *Mutter's* troubles, she'd decided she would quit after this photo shoot. Hudson would be in an agreeable mood from a successful session.

She pulled open the door to the studio, and as she strode inside, her stomach tightened.

Hudson stood behind his camera, snapping pictures of a model wearing a slim knit dress. Another catalog shoot. These were her least favorite.

Summer turned to her a moment before Hudson did. He scowled. "Debo, you're late. I was beginning to think you weren't going to show."

"I'm sorry. I had a hard time getting away, and I

missed my ride." It wouldn't matter anymore. She knew that after today she wouldn't be coming back.

Hudson stomped over to her and gripped her shoulders. "You need to decide what's more important. I count on you being here. When you leave me in the lurch, you hurt all of us." He swept his arm toward his assistants and the other models.

"I'm sorry. Do you want me to leave?"

"No. You're finally here. Go with Tina and Lindsey, and they'll get you ready. And, Debo, be ready when you come back." With his fingers pinched together, he drew his fingertips down in front of him from his head to his waist. "In here."

Hudson could be a little overdramatic.

She followed in Tina and Lindsey's wake.

Deborah sat uncomfortably as Tina brushed and worked with her hair. Was Tina being purposefully rough today? Or did Deborah just not want to be here today so every little thing bothered her?

Amos would have a fit if he knew where she was. The ache inside her chest wrenched tighter. She took a deep breath to clear it away. She needed this distraction. She was earning money for her future. She was doing nothing wrong.

Once transformed from head to toe and back out in the studio, she stood off to the side for Hudson to need her and give her instructions. She didn't have to wait long.

"Okay, Angela. Get into your next outfit." Hudson turned to Deborah, then motioned with a sweep of his hand for her to step in front of the white backdrop.

She obeyed and faced the camera.

Hudson looked through his camera on the tripod. "I want a neutral, content expression. Neither happy nor sad. Think of your face as a blank canvas, waiting for the right emotion to descend upon it."

A blank canvas? How was she supposed to achieve that? She tried to appear neither happy nor sad. Was she succeeding?

"No, no, no." Hudson stepped out from behind his camera. "Not distressed. Let's try something else." He moved back behind his camera and pointed over his head. "Pick a point behind me and think of something happy. Like ropes of diamonds."

Diamonds didn't make her happy.

"Or ice cream."

That was better, but it was still cold outside. Now, if it was the middle of summer, ice cream would make her happy.

"Or a new fur coat."

Hudson really had no clue what made Deborah happy, so she pictured the kittens in the barn. They were so adorable.

The camera lens clicked repeatedly. "Good. Keep that up."

Then she pictured the kittens scampering about. Suddenly, Amos was there, being the man about the farm. Doing all the chores a man normally did, with the kittens climbing on him.

"Perfect," Hudson said.

Hay had showered down around her, and Amos swooped her out of harm's way, and they tumbled into a pile of hay. He stared at her. Instead of him pulling away this time, her heart took control, and Amos inched closer and closer until he was a breath away—

"Debo!"

Deborah blinked and focused on Hudson standing in front of her.

His hand on her arm. "I got the shots. I don't know where you went, but it was absolutely perfect, beyond what I had hoped for."

Her face warmed at having allowed herself to think of Amos in such a way. It was a silly dream. Wasn't it?

"From that blush, I'll guess that there was a handsome guy in your daydream." Hudson gave her a knowing smile, winked and walked off.

She put her hands to her hot cheeks. He couldn't possibly know. He didn't even know about Amos.

When the session concluded, Deborah chickened out telling Hudson this was her last shoot. She slipped away unnoticed. She would have to figure another way to tell him.

She couldn't go on like this much longer.

The following week, when their house telephone rang, Deborah picked up the slim-line phone and took it to her *vater* in the living room.

"*Hallo?*" *Vater* paused, then said, "*Hallo*, Kathleen... Teresa would do better if you came here...Just me?" His features settled into a grim expression. "When?... I will come...*Danki. Auf wiedersehen.*" He hung up the phone.

Deborah released her breath. "What is it?"

"The doctor wishes to see me. Not your *mutter.*"

Deborah's insides tightened. Had the doctor found something wrong with *Vater* in his blood? "When must you go?"

"She can see me now. Would you tell Hannah and Lydia to come with me? And then ask Amos to hitch up the buggy?"

"I want to come, too."

Vater stared at her for a moment, then nodded. "I've

kept things to myself for too long. I thought I could ignore this, but I can't."

In the buggy, Amos drove, and *Vater* sat up front with him. Deborah sat in back with her two oldest sisters.

At the Amish clinic, Jessica Yoder welcomed them and asked them to take a seat in the waiting area.

The emptiness in the pit of Deborah's stomach kept her on her feet. She wanted to run out of there. She didn't want to hear whatever bad news the doctor had, but she *needed* to know. Or how else could she help *Mutter*?

Dr. Kathleen came out with Rebecca Beiler and her three-year-old son. "Make a follow-up appointment with Jessica."

Amos, standing beside Deborah, took her hand. "Everything will be all right."

Though startling at first, his warm, strong hand around hers comforted Deborah. She never wanted him to let go. "How can it be? *Mutter* is… There's something wrong with her. What if she has Alzheimer's disease?"

"Let's not invite trouble. Trust *Gott*." He gave her hand a squeeze and let go before anyone saw.

Deborah had thrilled at his touch, but now her hand felt oddly empty.

Dr. Kathleen faced the crowd and smiled. "Oh, my. I didn't expect so many of you. Come into my office. I'll grab a few more chairs."

Amos picked up one of the vacated chairs. "How many do you need?"

"If everyone is coming in, three—wait—four. And one to prop up Bartholomew's leg."

He hefted two straight-backed chairs.

Deborah grabbed one herself, and Dr. Kathleen carried the fourth.

Once everyone sat, Dr. Kathleen turned to *Vater*. "Are you sure you want so many present for your *frau's* diagnosis?"

Vater looked at each of his daughters and Amos. "My daughters help their *mutter* all the time. They should know what is going on with her. They'll help me remember what you say. Amos has been helpful, as well."

"All right."

Hannah cleared her throat. "Is it Alzheimer's disease?"

"Ne."

Dr. Kathleen looked directly at *Vater*. "I don't have enough information yet to make a final diagnosis, but I'm fairly certain it's not Alzheimer's. We do need to do more tests, but I'll give you my preliminary findings. As far as I can tell, Teresa has two issues. One is complicating the other."

Deborah shifted to the edge of her seat. If she scooted any closer, she'd land on the floor. She held her breath.

The doctor went on. "I believe Teresa might have what's known as Graves' disease. It's an immune system disorder that results in the overproduction of the thyroid hormone, known as hyperthyroidism." She put her hand on her throat. "The thyroid is located here. Hers doesn't seem enlarged. With more tests, we can know for certain."

"Is there a cure for it?" *Vater* asked.

"Not a cure, but it can be managed. There are a few medications, but I'm reluctant to recommend any of them."

"Because you aren't sure yet?"

"Ne. Because of Teresa's other condition. She's pregnant."

No one spoke. No one moved. It seemed as though no one dared to breathe lest it make this unbelievable news real.

Pregnant? *Mutter* was going to have another baby? Hannah and Lydia exchanged knowing glances.

"Her pregnancy is heightening the Graves' disease, causing the thyroid to produce more hormones than normal. This is why she seems worse when she's pregnant, because she is. Graves' can be the cause of the anxiety, shaking hands, forgetfulness, insomnia, as well as a host of other things. Many of the things in her medical history could be adding to her memory issues, as well."

Vater frowned. "Pregnant?"

"*Ja*. That's why I don't want to give her any medications just yet. Whatever she ingests, the baby receives. The only one I might be comfortable giving her while she's pregnant would be a beta-blocker, but I believe we can achieve similar results with natural methods. Graves' is hereditary. Mostly occurring in women under forty."

Mutter had turned forty not more than three months ago.

"I would like to draw more blood from all of you to test for Graves' specifically." Dr. Kathleen handed *Vater* a sheet of paper. "This is a list of natural things to do to help manage Teresa's condition. Because we are Amish, we already do most of the things they suggest—minimize stress, eat fresh fruits and vegetables, don't eat processed foods, as well as others. They are listed on that paper. Her natural diet and low-stress environment have been managing her Graves' without even knowing it, but she'll need to cut out all caffeine."

"Is *Mutter* going to be all right?" Deborah asked.

"I think so, with a little extra care and attention. I'd like to come by the house to give her the news myself and draw more blood from each of you to test for Graves'."

"What about the baby? Will it be all right? Will it have Down syndrome like Sarah?" Not that that would change anything. The baby would still be born, but the family could be better prepared.

"That's one of the tests I'll request to have them run at the hospital. We want to keep *mutter* and baby as healthy as we can."

The following day, Dr. Kathleen dropped by the house to give her diagnosis to *Mutter*. The whole family, as well as Amos, gathered in the living room.

Dr. Kathleen went around the room telling each person their blood type. She saved *Mutter* for last. "Your blood type is O positive. You might possibly have Graves' disease. It's not life-threatening. We just need to adjust some of your meals and habits. Also…you are pregnant, Teresa. Congratulations."

Mutter beamed, unaware of the emotional turmoil this was causing her and would continue to cause. Not just for herself, but for the whole family.

Miriam's voice held less enthusiasm than one normally would have. "I am so happy for you, *Mutter* and *Vater*."

Joanna expressed her pleasure, too.

Sarah clapped her hands, but she didn't likely understand she would have a baby sister or brother in a few months.

Naomi folded her arms and pouted. She would be receiving less attention in the future and wasn't happy about it.

Kathleen continued, "I'm ordering further tests at the hospital."

Mutter's broad smile disappeared in a flash, and she

shook her head. "*Ne*. I'm not going to the hospital. I don't like doctors." Fear etched the lines of her face.

Before anyone could think to stop her, Naomi said, "Kathleen's a doctor. *Doctor* Kathleen."

Mutter stared at Kathleen. Her eyebrows furrowed, and her lips twitched. "*Ne*. Kathleen is a friend and neighbor." Her face relaxed, and her whole demeanor calmed.

Several relieved breaths exhaled around the room, including Deborah's.

"That's right," Kathleen said. "I'm your friend, but because you're older, your pregnancy needs to be monitored more closely to keep the baby healthy and safe."

Mutter shook her head. "I won't go to the hospital."

Kathleen put a reassuring hand on *Mutter's* arm. "I can go and be with you every step of the way."

"*Ne*. I'm not going. I don't like doctors." *Mutter* stood and rushed into the kitchen.

Vater trailed after her on his crutches, followed by Hannah and Lydia.

Deborah had been excluded from too much of the family's goings-on. She would not be left out again and joined them. Amos came as well and stood in the doorway.

It took cajoling and comforting from *Vater*, Hannah, Lydia and even Amos to calm *Mutter* and convince her to go to the hospital for tests.

Deborah knew so little about *Mutter* and her condition to be of any use. That would not be the case next time. She would learn all she could about her *mutter's* condition to help her.

Chapter Thirteen

Deborah's sisters and *Mutter* bustled around the kitchen, preparing lunch. Deborah took the opportunity to sneak into the living room, where her *vater* sat with his leg up.

He spoke before she could. "I have had enough of sitting around." He rubbed his shoulder, the reason why he shouldn't use his crutches too much. The use of them had already slowed his shoulder healing.

"I'm sure you have." Deborah sat next to him and cast a glance toward the kitchen to make sure no one had decided to wander this way. She needed to speak quickly while she had him to herself. "*Vater*, I want to find natural alternatives to the prescription medications to keep *Mutter's* anxiety under control when she goes to the hospital. I would like your permission to go to the library in town after lunch and do some research. I won't use the computer myself. I'll have one of the *Englishers* do it for me. I'll see if I can check out a book about natural remedies, too."

Vater put on his thinking face of thinned lips and squinted eyes and remained quiet for a moment. "*Ja.* That would be *gut*. Also, go to the bookstore and purchase a book on natural remedies so we always have something here. I'll give you money. Amos will go with you. He can pick up my planting seeds and a few other things. Have Hannah make a list, as well. Don't tell *Mutter* or the younger ones. Send Amos in here so I can tell him."

A trip into town with just Amos. In spite of her worries about *Mutter's* conditions, Deborah's insides danced.

After lunch, she slipped outside unnoticed. Even with finally being included in the family secret, everyone overlooked her. This time she didn't mind.

Amos had Floyd partially harnessed to the wagon.

Deborah set her shopping bag with *Vater's* money and some of her own, along with a few more empty cloth shopping bags, on the floor of the wagon and helped. Soon, she sat on the seat next to Amos as they headed into town.

As the wagon lumbered down the road, she studied the man sitting next to her out of the corner of her eye. He seemed so comfortable at the reins. And why shouldn't he be? He had been born and bred Amish. He'd grown up at the reins. It wasn't that he looked comfortable so much as content. *Ja*, that was it. Content. Something Deborah had never been. Even from a young age, a restlessness had been inside her. She'd always yearned for more in life than rising early, working hard from sunup to sundown and going to bed at the end of the day. Though all *gut*, she sensed a different purpose for herself.

Dr. Kathleen had felt that pull, too. She'd gone out into the world, then had returned to help others. Deborah wanted that, too. But what purpose could she have? She didn't want to be a doctor, or go to school for years.

She shifted on the seat. "Do you think Dr. Kathleen was wrong to go into the *Englisher* world and become a doctor?"

"She is doing great *gut* for our community, so I don't see how that can be bad."

"But she left for so long. Our people believe that when a child of the Amish goes out into the world, they are turned over to the devil. That if they died out there, they wouldn't go to Heaven. Is that true?"

"I hope not."

"Because of your cousin Jacob?"

He hesitated before he answered. "Him and others. I'm not sure I see where living here or out there or anywhere changes what's in your heart. If you love *Gott*, you love *Gott*. He is not limited to one place or another but is everywhere."

"I like that. *Gott* is not limited."

"*Ja.* I like that, too. We shouldn't put restrictions on *Gott*." Amos pulled up in front of the library. "I'll leave you here while I go to the feed and seed stores."

Deborah climbed down. "About an hour?"

"Maybe a bit more."

"*Gut.* That should be plenty of time." She wanted to stay at his side and go everywhere he did. If she did that, there wouldn't be enough time to get everything done and return before supper, so she headed inside the library.

Deborah had lost track of time, and over an hour later, she peered out the front window of the library. She'd searched through many natural-remedy books and checked out three. One of the librarians had searched on the computer and printed off several pages of information for her.

Amos stood on the sidewalk, talking with a man,

and walked away from him. His cousin. The cousin who had been at the hospital the day *Vater* had gotten injured. The cousin who had come to the farm to talk to Amos. The cousin who had left the community. Deborah pushed open the door and trotted down the front walk to him. "Jacob, isn't it?"

He turned with a start, guilt contorting his face. Like a child caught taking a cookie before supper. *"Ja."* He glanced around.

"I'm Deborah. I live on the farm your cousin Amos is working on."

He swallowed hard. "It's nice to meet you. I'm Jacob—but you already know that. You know you could be shunned for speaking to me."

"Only if someone sees and tells one of the church leaders. Then I will confess my wrongdoing, be forgiven and not be shunned."

Chuckling, his body relaxed. "You like to live dangerously."

"I wouldn't call talking to you *dangerous*. Even if it were, I wouldn't say I *like* danger."

He smirked. "I'd say you like danger just a little bit."

How had this conversation gotten off the topic of why she'd come over here to talk to Jacob in the first place? She best get it out before things got off track again. "Is Amos planning to leave the community?"

He froze in midbreath, and his words squeaked out. "What? Why do you ask that?"

"Because *you* left, and I keep seeing you talking to him."

He hesitated. "We're still cousins. He lets me know how my family's doing."

Though she believed him, she felt there was more to this. "Don't make him leave."

"I can't *make* anyone do anything. It was nice talking to you." He walked around an old blue pickup truck and climbed in. He waved as he drove off.

An uneasiness coiled around Deborah's heart. Was Amos truly thinking about leaving? Was this why he'd said he hoped *Gott* was everywhere? Because he hoped *Gott* would be with him when he left?

The clomping of a horse's hooves brought her back to the present. Amos smiled at her from inside the buggy.

Ne, he wouldn't leave. Would he?

She climbed in.

"Discount store now?" Amos clicked out the side of his mouth and gave the reins a snap. Floyd plodded forward.

"Um." She shook away the thought of his potential leaving. For now. "I think there's a health-food store on the way. Can we stop? I want to get some things to try with *Mutter*." At the store, she spoke to a helpful employee and bought a homeopathic book. She also purchased some natural remedies for *Mutter*. Afterward, she completed Hannah's list at the discount store.

On the way out of town, Deborah pulled out the homeopathic book she purchased and flipped through the pages. How would she get *Mutter* to agree to take the remedies she'd purchased? Hannah would probably have a *gut* idea how best to approach the topic with her.

Amos leaned over and looked at the book. "Is all that safe for the baby?"

"Why wouldn't it be?"

"I don't know. I just know there are some foods we don't feed to young babies because their bodies can't digest them until they're older."

Amos posed a *gut* question. "You're right. Can we

stop in at Dr. Kathleen's, and I'll ask her? I don't want to risk *Mutter* or the baby."

Once at the doctor's office, the doctor scrutinized each of the remedies and searched in her own texts as well as thumbing through Deborah's books. "You've chosen well. These remedies all seem safe."

"*Danki.* I wanted to make sure before I gave *Mutter* anything."

"It is always *gut* to be safe. Let me know how she does on each of these. Start them one at a time to make sure she doesn't have a reaction. If she does, you'll know it's the newest one."

"*Danki.*" Deborah tucked the remedies back into her cloth shopping bag with the books.

Dr. Kathleen gave Deborah a pointed look. "Have you thought about studying homeopathy? Natural remedies."

"I don't want to be away to learn such things. My family needs me to help with *Mutter.*"

"You wouldn't have to leave. More and more studies are available online from home. I think you have a natural gift for it."

Deborah had enjoyed the research and learning. "Do you think the church leaders would allow that?"

"Times are changing. Our Amish needs have changed. Amish don't want to rely on *Englishers*, but we have to more and more. If we don't want to be dependent on the outside world, then some of us need to get more education than eighth grade, for the *gut* of the whole community. We must become self-reliant in some of these higher education areas. Just think about it, Deborah."

She would. She liked the idea of learning more about natural remedies and learning at home. She left with

Amos. The encounter with Jacob niggled in her mind. Should she ask Amos outright if he was going to leave? She wasn't sure she would like the answer. "Why do people abandon their Amish ways and go live in the *Englisher* world?"

"Um, uh… Why do you ask?"

"Oh, never mind." She shouldn't have said anything. She didn't want to know.

He turned sideways in the seat. "You asked earlier about Dr. Kathleen's actions. Now this. You aren't thinking of leaving, are you? Because that would be a bad idea."

Bad idea, indeed.

"Me? *Ne.* But people do it. Like your cousin and the bishop's granddaughter. Why do they turn their backs on all the beliefs they were raised with? Do they not believe in *Gott* anymore?"

He faced forward again. "I suppose they must have reasons they think are important enough. Maybe they are disillusioned with this life. That Amish aren't who they pretend to be. But as I said before, I believe *Gott* is everywhere."

That hit her square in her guilty heart. She had been pretending to be both Amish and an *Englisher* for a year, and felt torn between the two. But would she ever seriously consider leaving? She doubted it. "Why did your cousin leave?"

"He felt the *Englisher* world held more opportunities for him."

Was that what Amos was looking for? More opportunities? "What opportunities would be better than our Amish life?"

"I don't know. I guess they're just different."

So far, he hadn't given her an indication one way or

the other if he planned to leave. "What about you? Is there anything that would draw you to escape into the *Englisher* world permanently?"

"I don't know. I suppose if a person searched long enough, they could come up with something that made sense to them."

Her heart sank. How much more noncommittal could he be? He was searching for a reason to leave. Why couldn't he have said that *nothing* could ever make him leave?

Nothing.

At the farm, she left Amos in the barn to finish un-hitching and caring for Floyd. She had returned in time to help prepare supper. The task had never appealed to her before, but now that her family included her, she liked the camaraderie and connection with her sisters and *Mutter.*

She pulled Hannah aside. "I checked out three books from the library and bought one at the health-food store on natural remedies."

"We should ask Dr. Kathleen if these will be safe for the baby and for *Mutter.*"

"I stopped in on the way home. She said the ones I got would be fine."

Hannah hugged her. "*Danki.* You have done such a *gut* job. I'm sorry I ever doubted you could be of help."

Her sister's praise wrapped around Deborah like a prewarmed quilt. "How could you have known when I was never here?"

Dr. Kathleen's suggestion of learning more about natural remedies intrigued her and took root. She could not only help her *mutter,* but also others in her community. And somehow, she needed to convince Amos to stay.

The task of helping Sarah make biscuits fell to Deborah. And she had fun doing it. Sarah enjoyed most everything, unless she wanted her way and wasn't getting it, but in general, her baby sister was a joy. Soon they would have another little one running around the house.

At the kitchen sink, Deborah washed flour off her hands and glanced out the window. When she saw a shiny black Porsche pull into the driveway, her heart seized. *"Ne. Ne. Ne."* Hudson couldn't be here. She'd never told him where she lived.

"What's wrong?" *Mutter* sat at the table, turning pages of a cookbook.

"Nothing." Deborah shook water from her hands and grabbed a kitchen towel. "I'll be right back."

All of her sisters stared at her, but Hannah spoke. "Where are you going?"

"Outside. Be right back." Deborah raced out of the house in hopes of stopping Hudson before he got out of his car. She needed him to turn around and leave before anyone saw him.

But Hudson did get out and had closed his car door by the time Deborah reached him. She opened the door. "How did you find me? Get back in. You have to leave right now."

"It wasn't easy." Hudson closed the door again, leaned against it and pulled an envelope out of his inside jacket pocket. "Your latest wages. You never came to collect it."

Deborah took it. "Thank you. Bye."

He didn't budge. "You've missed a couple of photo shoots. I had to come to see if you were all right. You've put me in quite a bind, Debo."

She cringed at her modeling alias. It all seemed so silly now. How could she have ever thought that life was so *wunderbar*? This was as *gut* a time as any to tell him. "I'm fine. But I can't model for you anymore. Please go."

Hudson straightened, pushing away from the car. "You're quitting?"

"*Ja*. My *mutter* is ill. I'm needed here. Now, please go before anyone sees you."

He took her hand. "Debo, I can't let you go."

She pulled on her hand, but he held fast. "Don't call me that. You have to let me go. You have plenty of other models."

"No one like you."

She shook her head. "I know your other models get you the shots you need. I liked believing I was special, but I know now that I'm not."

He squeezed her hand. "You *are* special. You're special to me. I didn't keep using you on shoots just because you're beautiful and a good model. I didn't keep excusing your tardiness or not showing up because you're irreplaceable as a model. I did those things because you're irreplaceable to me. I care a lot about you. I hoped to come here to convince you to leave this simple life and be with me."

Two months ago, she might have considered his offer, but now it just sounded ridiculous, and not just because of her *mutter's* conditions. There was Amos, too. "Leave? I can't leave."

"Yes, you can. You could be so much more than this. You could be a star. I can make you a star. I know you love modeling. I've seen it in your eyes."

He was right. Modeling *had* sparked something inside her. Partly because his attention had made her feel special and partly because she was doing something forbidden. She felt sort of a thrill getting away with it, but it had been wrong.

"I did love it, but I can't do it anymore. My family needs me." And she needed her family. Modeling had been hollow. She could see that now. She'd welcomed her family into that empty space, and they brought her joy.

"Please consider my offer. I'll take care of you. I have a large apartment. There's plenty of room for you."

"Are you asking me to marry you?" That didn't sound like Hudson. He was not the commitment type.

"Not right away. Maybe in time."

Which most likely meant never.

"You expect me to leave my family, whom I could never come back to, to live with you? You don't know me at all." She hadn't known herself either, but now she did, at least a little better. And what she knew was that she was Amish and would always be Amish. Her family needed her, and she would be here for them. For a change.

"I thought you cared about me, too."

Deborah had basked in his praise, but she held no fondness for Hudson outside of modeling. She'd thought she did. She had even had a crush on him in the beginning. She could see now how shallow all that had been. "I'm not modeling ever again, and I'm not going to leave with you. My family needs me. I belong here. Goodbye, Hudson." She tossed the envelope back at him and walked away.

"Debo. Debo? Debo!"

At the name of her model persona, Deborah ran and didn't stop until she was back inside. She would never be Debo again.

"Who was that man?" *Mutter* asked.

Oh, dear. Her *mutter* had seen, and likely her sisters,

too. Had *Vater* seen? *Gott* willing, he had not. Hopefully, her *mutter* would forget as easily as she forgot Deborah. "No one. He lost his way." Both those statements were true. Hudson was no one to her anymore, and he'd lost his way because he never should have come out here.

Amos had watched Deborah run inside. What had that *Englisher* said to her to make her so upset? He strode over to the man in the dark suit who still stood beside his car. "What business do you have with Deborah?"

The man leveled his gaze at Amos and gave a sardonic laugh. "*Deborah?* You have no idea who she is. To me, she's Debo, the model. *My* model."

"Model?"

"That's having your picture taken with a purpose."

Why did *Englishers* think Amish didn't know anything about the outside world just because they chose not to get caught up in all those meaningless activities and collecting useless possessions? Sometimes *Englishers* were more ignorant than the Amish. But soon, *Amos* would be an *Englisher*.

The man went on. "In this case, catalogs and book covers. She's been modeling for me for over a year." He made his fingers do a walking motion. "Ever wonder where she sneaks off to? To see me." He poked his own chest with his index finger.

That couldn't be. Deborah couldn't be a model. She went to help a friend. Not to model. Deborah wouldn't do that. He studied the *Englisher*. *This* was the "friend in need" she slipped away to help so often?

"I asked her to come live with me. She's considering it."

Ne, Amos would *not* believe that. He wouldn't believe anything this *Englisher* said. "You need to leave." He narrowed his eyes.

"Admit it, you don't know your little Amish girl as well as you thought you did."

Anger rose up inside Amos. "Now."

The man opened his car door. "Tell Debo she hasn't seen the last of me." He got in and drove away, kicking up dirt and gravel. Once on the blacktop of the road, the car sped up and raced away with a thundering roar.

Amos picked up the envelope Deborah had tossed back at the man. The outside simply read "Debo." What was in it? Should he open it? Should he give it to her *vater*? He flipped it over. The flap hadn't been sealed down, just tucked inside. Deborah would never know if he peeked at the contents. He stared at it for a long time before he retreated into the barn and stowed it under his cot.

He would ask Deborah about this. She would tell him who that man was and what was really going on.

He strode to the house and entered through the kitchen door. All the women stood or sat, busy at tasks. "Deborah, may I speak with you?"

Sarah came over and hugged him around the waist.

Lydia put her hand on the little girl's shoulder. "Let him go."

Sarah did and smiled up at him.

He smiled back at her, then looked at Deborah.

She stared, unmoving, as though she might deny his simple request.

"Go on." Teresa waved for Deborah to comply.

She released the dishcloth in her hand and followed him outside. "What is it? I need to help with supper."

"Let's talk in the barn." He led the way, and once inside, he faced her. "Who was that man?"

Her gaze darted around as though she didn't know who he was talking about, but then she asked, "Who, the man in the black Porsche?"

She knew the kind of car? Had she ridden in it, as well?

He held up his hand. "Before you say anything else, wait here." He didn't want her to be tempted to lie. He went into his small room, returned with the envelope and held it up. "He told me you've been modeling for him."

Her face paled. "You spoke to him?"

"I did, but I didn't believe anything he told me. He called you Debo. I want to hear what you have to say about this."

She stared at him for a long time, then took a deep breath. "*Ja.* I did some modeling, but it wasn't anything bad. It was for high-end catalogs and book covers."

He stared back. That wasn't the answer he'd expected. He'd thought she would explain this whole thing away and paint a completely different picture. "Having your picture taken willingly like that is bad. He's the *friend* in need you've been helping?"

She bit her bottom lip. "Sort of."

Then it was true. "You know consenting to have your picture taken is forbidden."

Her voice came out small and frail. "I know."

"I can't believe you would do something so blatantly wrong." Just another Amish girl being duplicitous. Were there any who were trustworthy? What should he do now? "He said he asked you to go away with him and that you are considering it."

"*Ne!* He asked, but I would never do that. Never consider it."

Dare he believe her? Either she told the truth now and lied before, or she lied now and told the truth before. Either way, she'd lied to him. She had participated in an activity she knew went against their Amish beliefs. He held out the envelope. "What's this?"

She looked from him to the envelope and back to him before taking it. "Did you open it?"

"*Ne.* I thought about it, but it's yours."

"It's money for the work I did." Her voice sounded defeated. "I'm sorry I ever did it. I quit. I'm not modeling for him anymore. It's over." She stared at Amos a moment. "What are you going to do?"

The proper Amish thing to do would be to tell her *vater.* To tell the church leaders. But then a proper Amish wouldn't be making plans to leave. "I don't know."

"I promise I'm not going to model anymore. Ever again. I want to help take care of my *mutter.* And now with a new little one on the way, there will be a lot to do."

No wonder she was a mystery to him—she'd been harboring a secret. A huge secret. Maybe more. "Any more secrets I should know about?"

"*Ne.*" She chewed on her bottom lip.

He wanted to believe her but didn't know how with all her secrets and lies.

"Let me know what you decide to do." She walked away.

Part of him wanted to tell on her as quickly as possible to hurt her the way she'd hurt him, and then leave this farm to get away from her. Get away from this community. But another part of him wanted to keep her secret and protect her.

He cared about her more than he realized, and that made her betrayal of trust hurt that much more. How could he ever trust her again? He couldn't. He needed to leave as soon as possible. But could he leave her? His heart didn't want to.

Tears coursed down Deborah's cheeks as she ran through the field to the pond. The ducks squawked and flapped their wings to get out of her way. "Sorry." She plopped down on her sitting log.

How could she have been so stupid? The attention and praise Hudson had given her had been empty and worthless.

The look of disappointment and disapproval in Amos's eyes wrenched at her heart. What had she done? He would never trust her again. That hurt more than she thought it could. If she'd walked in a different direction, she never would have met Hudson. Never modeled. Never fallen into that temptation.

She tilted her head heavenward. "*Gott*, I am so sorry for what I have done. What do I do now?"

The image of banding together with her sisters, helping their *mutter*, flashed in her mind.

A peace washed over her soul, and a contentment she'd never felt before swirled inside her. A smile pulled at her mouth. She sensed the Lord calling her to care for her *mutter*. Deborah had a purpose now.

She stared at the crumpled envelope fisted in her hand. She'd forgotten about it. She didn't want this money or any of the money she'd earned. It was all tainted.

Standing, she wadded up the envelope with the enclosed money into a ball and prepared to throw it into the water. She stopped with her hand over her head, getting the impression to hold on to it. But why?

She flattened the rumpled envelope and folded it in half. She would need to figure out what *Gott* wanted her to do with this money.

Chapter Fourteen

Amos stewed for two days over Deborah's misdeeds. He should tell Bartholomew what she'd done. But that would hurt Deborah. But to not tell her *vater* would be a betrayal of the trust he'd placed in Amos, and a betrayal of the trust the bishop had placed in him. But Deborah would hate him if he told. But then, he'd betrayed them all by plotting his escape from the community.

He wanted to be away from her, but at the same time, not let her out of his sight. Even now that he knew her secret, he sensed there was so much more to learn about her. He didn't need to get tangled up with a duplicitous girl and her secrets. This twisting inside rattled him. Though he knew what he should do, he didn't want to do it.

He'd thought life on a farm with females would be easy, simpler. He couldn't have been more wrong. He should just get his departure over with instead of continuing to delay. He could see no other way out of this mess except to leave the community now. Before any of this mattered.

He headed to his little room in the barn. The kittens lay curled up in a huddle on his cot. He pulled out the cell phone. He'd thought he wanted to leave but now a part of him wasn't sure anymore.

Had it only been a week or two before Bartholomew's accident that he'd run into Jacob in town? His cousin had understood Amos's angst and betrayals. Had told him that *Rumspringa* wasn't a *gut* representation of actually *living* in the *Englisher* world. That he needed to try it. So, why not? The Amish world hadn't treated him very well, had ended up not having anything to offer him. No land to work or a trustworthy wife.

Amos sat on the other end of the cot from the kitten pile with the cell phone in his hands, weighing it as he weighed his options. He liked working on the Miller farm, felt at home here, but he couldn't stay indefinitely. Bartholomew would get his cast off soon. Amos couldn't return to his family's farm. What had he told Deborah? The *Englisher* world held different opportunities. He wouldn't know what those opportunities were until he tried. Right?

He pressed the button to turn on the phone. Nothing happened. He held down the button. Still nothing. Dead battery. He'd forgotten to plug it in all this time. He could charge it in the electrical outlet in the main part of the barn, normally used to plug in a heater to keep young or sick livestock warm on bitter winter nights. He dug the cord out from under the cot. Dare he charge it now?

The sound of female humming drifted into the barn.

He tossed the phone and cord under the cot. It hit the back wall with a thump. He cringed.

The humming grew louder, as one of the girls entered the barn. "Great Is Thy Faithfulness" floated through the air.

Deborah?

He stepped out of his room.

Miriam sucked in a breath, interrupting her tune.

Not Deborah. Just as well. "I'm sorry. I didn't mean to startle you."

She smiled. "My fault. I was deep in thought. Not paying attention."

Miriam *was* a sweet girl. No secrets. No disguise. No subterfuge.

Maybe he was drawn to enigmatic girls for a reason. But if he didn't want to be surprised or disappointed, he should find a girl who didn't hide behind a mask. But how would he know? "What brings you out here?"

She held up the shiny galvanized pail. "I'm on my way to milk Sybil."

Of course. He should have known. Quiet, dependable Miriam. Always doing her work without complaint. No mystery about her. Just what he needed.

But nothing about her appealed to him. Nothing drew him in. Nothing made him want to know more. Was there anything more to know?

Not like Deborah, who had an alluring mystique about her.

And secrets.

The following week, Deborah helped her *mutter* on with her coat. *Mutter* had scheduled tests at the hospital today, and *Vater* was taking her, accompanied by Hannah and Lydia, who had been the most involved in *Mutter's* management.

The anxiety remedies Deborah had purchased in conjunction with avoiding caffeine seemed to keep *Mutter* amenable. Deborah prayed the calm lasted. Mostly for *Mutter's* sake so she wouldn't be frightened, but also for the others looking after her.

The foursome headed out the door, followed by Deborah and Miriam.

Amos stood out front with his hand on Floyd's bridle. Her emotions fluttered about from one to another and back. First happy to see him, then guilty for her secret, then dread that he would tell someone mixed with relief he hadn't. Maybe she needed some of those remedies to calm her nerves.

He had avoided Deborah since the Hudson incident, showing up only at mealtimes and leaving shortly afterward. As far as she could tell, he hadn't told her *vater* about her having modeled. She was afraid to ask what he decided to do with the information, fearful it would push him into telling *Vater* and others what she'd done.

Right now, she couldn't brood over what he *might* do.

Amos held open the buggy door and spoke to *Vater*. "I can drive if you like."

"*Danki*, but I will feel better to have a man on the farm while I'm in town. We will probably be there most of the day."

Deborah stepped forward. "I could go and help out."

"I think too many people going might make *Mutter* more nervous than she already is. Even though the herbs you purchased seem to be helping. We'll tell you everything we learn."

She ached to go, but agreed it was probably best if she didn't. "Are you picking up Dr. Kathleen on the way?"

"*Ne*. She's meeting us at the hospital."

"Don't forget to tell her how the remedies are working so far."

"I will, little *mutter* hen." *Vater* patted Deborah's hand and climbed in the back with *Mutter* and situated his crutches.

Hannah, at the reins, drove away.

As they left, Deborah's heart weighed heavy.

Amos came up beside her. "Your *mutter* is going to be all right."

Surprised, she turned to him. The first words he'd spoken to her in days. Words of comfort, no less. "You're speaking to me again?"

He gave her a weak smile but didn't answer her question. "Your *vater* and sisters will take *gut* care of her."

That was part of the problem. They *always* took care of *everything*, unintentionally excluding Deborah to the point she wasn't needed. But *she* had been the one to find the natural remedies, and that made her feel better. "*Danki* for being here to help us in all of this."

"I'm glad I could, but I haven't done very much."

"Oh, but you have. Just being here to support us and keeping our secret. At least for now." Deborah knew how to keep secrets. And now Amos knew hers. How long would he keep it? "Unless the doctors can figure out exactly what's wrong with her and make her better, I think a lot more people are going to find out about her conditions."

"That won't be so bad, will it?"

His concern touched her, especially after so long a silence. Was his talking to her a sign that he'd made a decision?

"It depends on how they react."

He nodded. "True. Even in our community people can be unkind without realizing it."

"Especially children. They may not mean to be, but words could be out of their mouths before anyone can stop them." Deborah hoped no one spoke cruelly to, or about, *Mutter*.

In the late afternoon, Amos tinkered with the tractor, making sure it was in *gut* working order to plow soon. The kittens climbed all over the tractor and him, investigating his work.

Deborah lingered in the barn with him so she would know as soon as her parents and twin sisters returned. Several clip-clopping false alarms had sent her rushing outside. Still no sign of them. "Sooo…you haven't said anything to my *vater* about my modeling. Does that mean you've decided not to?" Her fear of pushing him into an action that would have repercussions for her still coiled inside her, ready to strike. Why had she asked now? Because the tension between them needed something to defuse it. That *something* could be nothing other than his decision. Also, his not speaking to her bunched up her insides even more. Besides, not knowing what he would do weighed on her.

"And here I thought you liked my winning company."

Well, she did, but she couldn't tell him that. His words had held a hint of hurt and bitterness. "Never mind. I shouldn't have asked."

He stared at her a moment as though he wanted to say something, then turned back to the tractor, and then back to her. "I'm still having a hard time believing you modeled. You aren't the person I thought you were. I thought I knew you, but I was wrong."

That stabbed her heart. She was disappointed in herself, as well. Should she let the topic drop? Or explain herself? She hated having Amos think poorly of her. "I didn't know who I was. I thought I was an Amish girl waiting for the rest of her life to begin. I thought my family didn't understand me or care. I thought I needed someone to tell me nice things to feel worthy." Was she only making it worse with her self-centered selfish words?

"And now?"

"You don't want to hear me ramble on."

"I actually do. You thought you needed someone to make you feel worthy. And now?"

"I'm not sure, but I know modeling will never make me feel worthy. That's not the kind of worth I need or want. I was an Amish girl living outside my own life. Instead of including myself as a part of my family, I waited for my family to include me. I excluded myself and blamed them. That probably sounds foolish to you."

"Needing to feel like you matter is important."

The quality in his voice made her wonder. "You understand needing to feel like you matter, don't you?"

"I've had my share of disappointments."

Was that why he was going to turn his back on his whole way of life? Dare she ask him? "Disappointments? Here or back in Pennsylvania?"

"Both."

So he was including her.

He pointed with a wrench he'd been using on the tractor toward the large open doorway.

"What disappointments?"

"I think I hear them coming back."

She listened and heard the faint clomping of a horse's hooves. How had he heard that so much sooner than her? She dashed out as the buggy turned into the driveway.

Lydia, at the reins, drove the buggy to the front of the house and stopped.

Hannah jumped out with her finger to her lips. "Shhh. *Mutter* and *Vater* fell asleep on the ride home."

Deborah peered through the window into the back.

Vater's arm encircled *Mutter's* shoulders. Her head lay on his shoulder, and his head rested on hers. He loved *Mutter* so much, regardless of what was happening and all that had happened with her.

Would Deborah ever find an unconditional love like that? Not with Amos. She'd disappointed him. Her parents had something rare. 'Twas true that Amish always took care of their own, but sometimes grudgingly. Not so with *Vater*. He happily cared for *Mutter*.

Miriam came out of the house.

Lydia stepped down from the buggy. "Hannah, I'll make sure the others stay inside while you tell Miriam and Deborah what we learned."

Hannah kept her voice low and pointed toward the horse. "I'll talk while we unhitch Floyd."

Amos helped Deborah on one side while Hannah and Miriam worked the harness on the other side.

Deborah rose up on tiptoe and peered over Floyd's back at Hannah. "What did you find out?"

"First, *danki* for finding those remedies. They helped *Mutter* a lot. She remained calm most of the time. She had a few nervous episodes, but *Vater* was able to assuage her fears. She's indeed pregnant. We spoke to many, *many* doctors, including a psychiatrist. They confirmed that she has Graves' disease. They all believe that her pregnancy is aggravating it. They also discovered scar tissue on her brain, likely from the buggy accident when she was three. It traumatized her, and that, compounded by multiple surgeries when she was young, is causing some of her memory issues and other problems."

"Poor *Mutter*."

"The psychiatrist thinks that some of her memory issues are actually her regressing to a younger age as a way of coping. He would like to see her weekly."

"Is she going to go?"

"I don't know. No one in our community has ever gone to a psychiatrist. *Vater* would need to get permission from the bishop. I doubt he would give it. Plus, I don't think *Vater* wants to have her going to an *Englisher* doctor every week."

"Why doesn't she just go to Dr. Kathleen? Bishop Bontrager would approve that."

"Dr. Kathleen is a different kind of doctor."

"Did they give her medications to help her symptoms?" Deborah asked.

"*Mutter* and *Vater* agreed that they didn't want to expose the baby to medications if they didn't have to. Dr. Kathleen is going to monitor *Mutter* closely."

"Is the baby all right? Does it have Down syndrome like Sarah?"

"We don't know. When *Mutter* found out that the amniocentesis test had any risk at all, she refused. She became very agitated, and we had a hard time calming her back down. Whatever we found out wouldn't matter. The baby is already who she's going to be with a strong heartbeat. We'll love her no matter what."

"She? Is it a girl?"

"We don't know for sure, but chances are it will be. We all got to see the new little one on an ultrasound."

"When's the baby due?"

"August. From the ultrasound, they think she's around sixteen weeks."

If Deborah and her sisters could manage *Mutter* for the next five months, through her pregnancy, then once the baby was born, she would naturally improve. In the meantime, Deborah would hire an *Englisher* to do more research on the computer. She would find whatever natural treatments would help *Mutter* best, and use her modeling money for that.

That evening, Deborah sat at the kitchen table with her *vater* and three older sisters. *Vater* devised a rotating schedule among the five of them to keep an eye on *Mutter*. *Vater* would take charge of her in the evenings and through the night. Hannah would oversee *Mutter* first in the morning, then Lydia, then Miriam and then finally Deborah up to and through supper.

Deborah pointed to her twin sisters. "But what about in the fall when Hannah and Lydia marry?"

Lydia piped up. "I won't marry. I'll always stay here and take care of *Mutter*."

Mutter would likely need close supervision the rest of her life.

"I'll stay, too," Hannah said.

Then Miriam spoke. "No need for the two of you to give up on marrying. You both have *gut* men who want to marry you. I'll stay with *Mutter*."

"Don't *you* want to marry?" Hannah asked.

"Knowing *Mutter* needed supervision, I've never truly believed I could. I've tried to keep boys from being interested in me so I could remain single."

Deborah's spirit lifted, then fell. "*Ne*, Miriam. I'll take care of *Mutter*. You—as well as Hannah and Lydia—have already done your fair shares. It's my turn to care for her."

"It would be *gut* if you all marry. Your *mutter* is going to need a lot of medical care in the next few months. It's going to be expensive. I may need to sell the farm. My mind will rest easier knowing you each have a home."

Deborah gasped in unison with her sisters. "*Ne, Vater*. Say it isn't so."

Vater let out a dejected sigh. "I will speak to the bishop, but I don't have much hope."

Before anything more could be said, *Mutter* entered the kitchen, and the conversation stopped.

Mutter looked around the table. "Bartholomew, you didn't tell me we had company. You ladies must think me a terrible hostess."

Deborah and her sisters exchanged glances with each other, then with *Vater*.

Vater spoke up. "We're all fine. No need to fuss. Sit."

Mutter sat. "I don't normally take a nap." She'd fallen asleep in the living room rocking chair right after supper. "But..." She leaned forward with a twinkle in her eyes. "We're expecting our first child."

Deborah's jaw went limp. First?

"If it's a girl, we're going to name her Hannah, and Micah for a boy."

Deborah glanced at her oldest twin as tears stung her eyes. Poor Hannah. It was so hard watching *Mutter* like this. Deborah preferred it when she had been blissfully ignorant. But there was no going back. She couldn't unlearn everything she knew now.

Vater gave *Mutter* a sad, weary smile. "These ladies already know. They came to see how they could help you. They are each going to take turns coming over and doing what they can."

Mutter smiled. "*Danki.* You are all so kind."

Each of her sisters said that they were glad to help, but there must be something more that Deborah could do. But what?

Chapter Fifteen

In the Millers' living room sat a pile of books. The one on the top caught Amos's attention. An Amish romance novel. Such silly books. Why did women like to read that nonsense? Especially practical Amish women. Didn't the Amish pride themselves on being separate from the world? Not to be just like them but without conveniences?

He picked it up and read the back cover. He still couldn't see the appeal. He turned it over and studied the profile image of an Amish woman looking down at a yellow flower with a dark center. He scrutinized the cover. Not just an Amish woman—Deborah! He wouldn't have believed it to be her if not for her confession to him.

Multiple footsteps thunked on the kitchen floor. The women had returned from visiting a neighbor.

He tucked the book under his arm and slipped out the front door. He took charge of the horse and buggy and walked the pair to the barn. Leaving Floyd hitched, he hurried to the safety of his room and stared at the cover again. Definitely Deborah. What should he do with this?

He knew Deborah had been modeling, but she said

she'd quit. She could get in trouble for this. He hadn't told Bartholomew or anyone else about her modeling and had no plans to at this point. To do so would be duplicitous, considering his own plans, as well as hurt Deborah. She would be angry with him. That bothered him more than her breaking the rules of the *Ordnung*.

He had work to get done before it was time to eat.

At supper that night, Amos ate with a guilty conscience. He knew he should give the book to Bartholomew and tell him what he knew about Deborah's modeling. But what about himself? He, too, harbored a secret. Guilt on top of guilt. Even after the hurt she'd caused him with her subterfuge, he still wanted to protect her. He was attempting to get away from duplicity in others, so he wouldn't stoop to it himself.

Miriam took a drink of milk. "Has anyone seen the novel I was reading? I left it in the living room, but it's gone."

"What's your book about?" *Mutter* asked.

"It's an Amish romance. *Amish Identity*. It's not really mine." Miriam turned to Deborah. "I hope you don't mind that I borrowed it."

Deborah's face turned ashen, and a slight tremor laced her words. "Um…I actually haven't finished with it myself."

Amos should probably say something, but he wanted to talk to Deborah first.

Vater swallowed his bite and pointed with his table knife. "I'm not so sure I like you girls reading those. They give you false ideals. Then you expect this romance nonsense that isn't practical in everyday life."

Mutter giggled. "*Ne*. They don't. The stories are all made-up. They're just *gut* fun. It's nice to take a break once in a while. Let the girls have their little escapes.

They always get their work done. Our girls are too smart to be swayed by stories."

Amos imagined that Deborah wished that her *vater* would forbid romance novels.

Bartholomew nodded. "Very well. Just be sure to get your work done."

All the girls around the table smiled except Deborah. Her ashen complexion had paled even more.

After supper, Amos came up beside Deborah and whispered, "May I talk to you?"

"I can't. I need to find my book Miriam *borrowed*."

"It's in the barn." He walked away, knowing she would come.

She snagged her coat and followed him out. "You have my book?"

"I saw it in the living room. I took it out to the barn."

She fell into step with him. "I can't picture you reading Amish romances."

He stopped. "*Ne.* I took it because *you* are on the cover."

Her eyes widened. "You recognized me?"

He proceeded to walk again. "It wasn't hard."

She trotted to catch up. "Do you think Miriam recognized me?"

"She didn't act as though she did." He went into his room and reached underneath his cot. He grabbed the novel but could feel the cell phone on top of it. He tried to shake the device off as he pulled the book out, but they both came. He dumped the phone onto the floor. In a single motion, he stood, kicked the phone back under the cot, turned and thrust out the paperback. "Here it is." Hopefully, she hadn't noticed the phone.

She stared at the floor near the cot for a moment longer before looking up at him. "*Danki*. I appreciate you not telling anyone about this."

If he exposed her secret, he would need to confess his own. "I thought you said you didn't have any more secrets."

"This isn't a different secret. It's part of the same one. I said I had modeled for catalogs *and* book covers." She tapped the front. "Book cover."

True. It had just been such a shock to see her like that. "You know that there are more copies of this out there? What happens when one of your sisters or someone else in the community picks one up and realizes that's you on the cover?"

"I don't know. Hudson took these shots on the very first photo shoot I did. I never imagined seeing myself on the cover of a book. It's so strange." She tilted her head. "You look as though you're the one who should feel guilty. I really have quit."

Keeping her secret wasn't the root of his guilt—keeping his own was. He couldn't risk anyone trying to talk him out of his decision.

Now that Bartholomew's cast was off, Amos wouldn't be needed for much longer. He would stay on until Bartholomew regained the strength in his injured leg. The young man, Jesse, who was supposed to have left by now had lost the place he was to move to. Whether he was gone or not, when it was time to leave the Millers', Amos wouldn't be returning to his parents' farm. It would be too hard to leave if he did.

Having spent the previous week making sure the fields were properly planted had given Amos a sense of great accomplishment. Not being around to reap the harvest of his labor caused sorrow and disappointment to roll through him. He would be leaving soon, but surprisingly, a part of him didn't want to anymore. He didn't want to leave the Millers' farm or Deborah. He felt at home here and wanted to stay.

Surprising revelation.

"Since you haven't said anything yet, does that mean you've decided not to tell anyone my secret?"

Ja, but it might be best not to let her know that yet. "I'm not sure." Once he was gone, she would know her secret was safe.

"My resolve to not model is solid. I won't ever do it again."

He believed her, but was it because he truly did or only because he *wanted* to. If he could, he would wrap her in his arms and protect her.

Alone in the room she shared with Miriam, Deborah tucked the book between the mattress and box springs and sat on her bed. She wished Miriam hadn't discovered her book. She would no doubt ask about it again. Deborah had almost forgotten about the damaging evidence, having tucked it away *under* her bed. Obviously, not a *gut* place. She should have set it afire in the burn barrel, then Miriam wouldn't have discovered it. She and her sisters often borrowed things from each other, many times without asking. Deborah would figure out a time when she could dispose of this copy.

Amos had been right. Numerous copies of this novel undoubtedly floated around out in the *Englisher* world, and likely, a few in their community. Who else held a copy? Then there were the other books that could potentially have a picture of her, as well. It would be only a matter of time before someone else discovered her secret. Should she ask Hudson to not sell any more of her pictures for covers? To destroy all the pictures he took of her? The thought of talking to him again gave her shivers. That he thought she would go with him to New York had been preposterous. *Ne.* Talking to Hudson would be a bad idea. A clean break was best.

Then what could she do? How long before someone else recognized her?

She would sleep on it.

But sleep evaded her, so she lifted her troubling situation to the Lord.

Gott, *what should I do? I could confess to my family, but that would hurt everyone, and they would be disappointed in me. There's a* gut *chance no one will ever find out, and then no one would get hurt. But the not knowing if someone will discover my secret is agitating. Tell me what to do.*

Vater had told the bishop and church leaders about *Mutter's* conditions. They in turn brought the concern before the congregation. Several families had recently experienced hardships, some with crops, others with medical expenses, and one family's house and barn had burned to the ground. There wasn't extra money in the community right now to cover so many needs. Maybe in a year or two things would be different, but *Mutter* and her family needed help now. The women did offer to take turns sitting with Teresa for a few hours each day to ease the burdens on her daughters.

But the future of the Miller farm was in jeopardy. They couldn't lose their livelihood. There must be something more Deborah could do to help.

The book cover flashed in her mind, and she thought of Hudson. That was it. She could continue to model, earning money to pay the doctor bills. But her declaration to Amos about never modeling again played in her head. Taunting her. This was the path she'd set herself on over a year ago. This was how she could help her family. Apparently, her desire to be the one to stay with *Mutter*, and also learn about homeopathy, so her sisters could marry would have to wait. Her family needed money now, but not for her to dally with natural remedies and sit with her *mutter* when there were others who could do that.

Deborah grabbed the telephone from the small table by the front door and slipped out onto the porch, pulling the door most of the way shut on the cord. She called for a ride from an *Englisher.* It took only a couple of calls before she found someone willing to pick her up within a half an hour.

Thankfully, Amos wasn't on watch at the moment, and she slipped away and across the field without any trouble. Once in town, she changed into jeans and a sweatshirt, let down her hair and walked to her destination.

She opened the door to the photography studio. The excited—and frustrated—voices of Hudson and Summer collided with each other and bounced off the cement walls. Deborah strolled inside to the sight of Hudson packing his camera gear in their hard-shell cases. Now that the weather was getting nicer, he must be preparing for a shoot outside in lieu of using one of his nature backdrops. She would take any job. Work six days a week if that was what it took to save the farm.

"Hallo?" Deborah called.

Hudson swung around toward her and frowned. "You? What do you want?"

She wouldn't be deterred by his foul mood. "I was hoping you had a modeling job for me."

He folded his arms. "I thought you quit. Never going to model again."

"I changed my mind."

"Why? You and that man on your farm were both pretty adamant."

She'd hoped he wouldn't ask, just be happy she was back. "My *mutter* needs some medical treatments. It's going to cost a lot. I need to earn money to help pay for it."

Summer pointed over her shoulder. "I'll see what needs to be packed in the back."

Hudson unfolded his arms and crossed the room to Deborah. "So, you're desperate."

She hadn't wanted to use that word, but it fitted. "In a way."

"The only job I have, you won't be interested in." He held out his hands. "Sorry."

"Why not? I'll take anything."

"Really? It's in New York City." He tapped his chest with the fingertips of both hands. "I finally got my break. I'm going to be famous."

"New York?"

He narrowed his eyes. "You desperate enough to come? You could be famous, too. It'll easily pay two or three times what any of us were making here."

She didn't care about being famous, but she needed the money. Two or three times more? Her family wouldn't have to worry about the medical bills. But leave Indiana? Leave her family? New York would mean no more running across the field to a photo shoot during the days and spending the evenings with her family. She would have to choose between the two.

"You said you'd take *anything*."

"I don't know." This was a much bigger decision than

simply modeling. She'd have to leave behind her whole life and take up a new one. There would be no coming back. Could she sacrifice everything for her family, who never noticed if she was there? They certainly wouldn't miss her. "Give me time to think about it."

"No time. I'm leaving in the morning, and I need to know if I'm to save room for you in the van."

If she didn't go, her family would lose everything. If she went, *she* would lose everything. To choose modeling *was* to choose her family and vice versa. She'd thought Hudson had been ridiculous for suggesting she go with him the day he'd come out to the farm, and now that was exactly what she was contemplating. Her short-lived dream of learning homeopathy would die today. She'd been raised to think of others before herself, to be selfless. She hadn't been doing either of those lately. Her life would change one way or another. She might as well make the change count for something. "I'll go to New York."

His eyes widened. "Seriously? I didn't think you would, but I'm *really* glad you are. You don't need to take anything from your Amish life. We'll get you all new clothes and anything else you need. We need to pack up all my photography gear."

Tears blurred her vision. "I need to go say goodbye to my family."

"Don't cry. It's not like you can't come back and visit."

But she couldn't. She would never see her family again. She would miss her family, and the community, too. A large part of her would miss Amos. But wasn't he going to leave anyway? Leave her behind? So, whether she stayed or not, he would be gone. "I'll be back in the morning."

* * *

Amos stood on the corner, waiting for Jacob in Goshen. He'd texted his cousin that he was ready. Just when he'd thought that there might be *one* Amish girl who wouldn't disappoint him, he'd been wrong. How could he have allowed himself to get emotionally tangled up with another female? Women caused chaos wherever they went. Life had been simpler on a farm with all males. Except his *mutter*.

Deborah, in *Englisher* clothes, strolled out of a building. Star Photography Studio.

She'd promised she quit. Promised to never go back. Just like a woman to go back on her word.

Not this time.

She headed off in the opposite direction from him.

He hustled after her and almost caught up to her and was about to call out when she entered a gas station/convenience store. He went inside but couldn't see her. Where had she disappeared to?

"Hey, Mr. Amish man?"

Amos swung around to the cashier behind the counter. Was he talking to Amos?

The young man inclined his head toward the back. "She's in the restroom, changing."

Amos stepped over to the counter. "Who?"

"That Amish girl. She comes in sometimes when I'm working. She goes in dressed like an Amish and comes out looking normal, then later in the day, she goes in normal and comes out Amish. But this time was weird. She was only gone for twenty minutes or so. Usually, it's hours."

So, she changed her clothes here. "Thank you." He went outside to wait and sat on the curb.

Ten minutes later, she exited and walked right past him.

He stood. "Deborah."

She spun around.

"Or should I call you Debo?"

"What are you doing here?"

Even now, with her new betrayal, he wanted to take her into his arms. Instead, he closed his hands into fists to keep himself from reaching out for her. "I could ask you the same thing, but I already know. I saw you come out of the photography place. You promised you'd quit modeling and never go back."

"I have no choice. My *mutter's* medical expenses will cost too much. My *vater* will have to sell the farm to get her the help she needs."

Excuses. "I was foolish enough to think you were different. I was going to ask you to leave with me, but didn't because of your emphatic declaration of quitting."

"Leave? So, you're in town to meet up with your cousin, never to return home. This whole time on our farm, you've been plotting your departure. I'm leaving to help my family. What's your excuse?"

Because he couldn't trust her or anyone, but that wasn't exactly true. He didn't want to risk trusting for fear he'd be hurt again. Was that a *gut* reason to leave?

Tears filled her eyes. "I'll miss you, Amos Burkholder." She turned and walked away.

He wanted to call her back. Shake some sense into her. Wrap her in his arms. He did none of those. Instead, he strolled back to the corner, where Jacob waited.

Deborah walked the whole way home from town. Two hours gave her a lot of time to think. Though she'd wanted to be the one to stay at home and take care of her *mutter*, it seemed as though the only way she could take care of her *mutter* and family was to leave them. She could make *gut* money modeling and pay for the medical bills that were already mounting up.

She ran into the house and up the stairs. She knew what needed to be done. She grabbed her tin of money and the novel with her on the cover. Back downstairs, she hurried outside. She'd seen her *vater* in the barn. She headed inside the shadows of the yawning opening. *"Vater?"*

He limped out of Floyd's stall. "Ah, Deborah. Sad news. Amos has left us. It was time for him to go home."

Home? Hardly. But that wasn't why she had come. *"Vater,* I have some *gut* news." She opened her tin. "This is for *Mutter's* medical expenses. I'm going to be able to pay for the rest of them, too."

He took her offered tin. "How? Where did this money come from?" He shifted his gaze back up to her. "There's so much."

"I earned it." She bit her bottom lip.

"Doing what? You don't have a job."

She swallowed down her guilt and fear. "I actually do. I've been working in town. That's where I would go all the time when I went for a walk."

"Why did you keep it a secret?"

She held out the Amish novel. "I've been modeling. This is me on the cover of this book."

He took it. "This is wrong, Deborah. It's forbidden to have your picture taken. This is a graven image. You must stop at once."

"I know. I did stop, but..."

"But you continue?" The hurt in his eyes stabbed at her heart.

"I have to. I can pay for *Mutter's* medical bills."

"*Ne.* I forbid it."

Tears blurred her vision. "I don't want our family to lose the farm."

"We will survive this. *Gott* will take care of us."

"*Ja.* And He's going to use me to do it. I'm leaving in the morning for New York City. I'll send all the money I make."

He shook his head. "*Ne.* I won't accept it."

Then she would pay the hospital directly.

"You must stay."

"*Ne.* If I go, I can help the family."

"You're just going to leave us?"

She nodded, afraid her voice would fail her.

Tears rimmed his eyes. "What am I supposed to tell the rest of the family?"

It touched her that he cared so much. She'd never seen him this emotional. "Tell them whatever you want. Tell them I've lost my way." She choked on every untrue word. "Tell them I've chosen the world over them."

"What about your *mutter*?"

"Don't you understand? I'm doing this for her. For all of you."

"If she could understand all that was going on with herself, do you think she would want you to do this for her?"

Ne. "This is the way I can help. Help her. Help you. Help the whole family."

"Where do I tell her you've gone?"

"She probably won't even notice. She'll forget she ever had a daughter named Deborah. It's best that way."

"Is that why you're doing this? You feel overlooked?"

Being overlooked was the reason it had been so easy for her to start modeling. She did it now because she loved her family too much to see them suffer.

If she'd paid more attention, maybe she would have realized something had been amiss. Words poured out that she couldn't stop. "When I was younger, I felt as though I was getting away with something and to get out of work." There had been a thrill in that. "Then, well... because no one noticed me, whether I was here or not. Naomi claimed as much of everyone's attention as she could. It didn't seem worth it to compete with her. If I wasn't here, I wasn't as hurt that no one paid attention to me. You all *couldn't* notice me if I was absent, then it wouldn't be because no one cared. I felt..."

Vater's voice came out sad and full of compassion. "Alone and unwanted?"

How had he known? *"Ja."*

Vater looked sad. "I'm sorry I made you feel that way. You are neither alone nor unwanted. Each of my girls is a precious gift from *Gott.*"

Deborah didn't feel like a gift. "Do you ever wish one of us had been a son who could help you more with the farmwork?"

"I always hoped to have a son, but I would never trade one of you girls for a son."

"Not even Naomi?" She shouldn't have said that. It popped out on its own accord.

He smiled. "Not even Naomi."

She suddenly realized that Naomi probably acted out for the same reason Deborah had withdrawn from the family—lack of attention. If either of them had known *Mutter* had problems, maybe neither would have taken the paths they did. But Deborah's path was set. She took her *vater's* hand. "I need to do this. I'll be able to pay the medical bills. You can keep the farm."

"I would rather have my whole family than the farm."

"You need the farm to support the family. Without it, what would become of everyone?"

"*Gott* will take care of us."

"Maybe *Gott* sent me to that first photo shoot as a way to take care of my family."

"Don't do this."

"It's already done."

"Then undo it."

She wanted to, but that wouldn't help anyone. "I'll leave first thing. Don't tell anyone until I'm gone."

"The morning? Then I still have time to pray for you."

It wouldn't do any *gut*.

She'd once looked forward to modeling. Not anymore. It was a burden she must bear.

Chapter Sixteen

In the predawn light, Amos drove his cousin's pickup along the country roads. He still had a current driver's license from when he was on *Rumspringa*. Granted, it was from Pennsylvania, but still *gut* for another six months. And he had liked cars—fast cars—as a lot of Amish boys did, but gave them up when he joined church.

The truck's engine suddenly chugged to a stop, and he lost the power steering. He cranked the wheel hard and coasted the vehicle to the shoulder. After several failed attempts to restart it, he jumped out and walked. Still a *gut* three miles to the Millers', he hoped he got there before Deborah left for New York City.

He'd joined church back in Pennsylvania so he could ask Esther to marry him. After courting for two years, she'd turned him down and married someone else that same year.

Now history was repeating itself. He'd become Amish for a girl, and now he would stay Amish for a girl.

Something pricked his heart. Was he only Amish to

please this girl or that? His parents? The church leaders? Were any of those *gut* reasons?

As he approached the Millers' house, the sun peeked over the eastern horizon.

Teresa Miller stood at the end of the driveway, looking back and forth.

He hurried up to her. "Teresa, what are you doing out here?"

She twisted one hand in the other and shook her head. "Why am I here?"

She must be having a bad day.

He took her hands in his. "Why don't we go up to the house?"

"I forget things." Teresa blinked several time in rapid succession. "I'm not well. I know that. But I'm not *un*well. Does that make sense?"

"*Ja.* But you're doing much better."

Her eyes brightened. "Am I?"

"*Ja.*" All the natural treatments and changes in her diet had improved Teresa's Graves' symptoms. She would never be like everyone else, but she would be functional. She would always need someone to watch over her. And she would always have loved ones to do that.

"You are a *gut* boy." She squeezed his hands. "Promise me something."

He wasn't really in a position to promise anyone anything. "If I can."

"Don't ever leave us."

His heart ached for her. He'd already done just that. "I wish I could promise you that." He truly did. "But I can't. The bishop has told me to return to my parents' farm." He felt bad for telling her that when he had already left the community. True, no one knew yet. The

Millers thought he'd gone home, and his family thought he was still at the Millers'.

"Oh, but you can't. You must stay. Here. With us. I'll have my husband talk to the bishop. I feel better because you're here. You help Bartholomew. He needs another man here. Too many women. We need you. He needs you. I need you."

What could he say to that? His heart cried out, *Ja, I'll stay.* Then he could continue to see Deborah every day—*if* he could convince *her* to stay.

"You're the one who found me on the road that day, aren't you?"

She remembered that? *"Ja."* He wished he knew then what he knew now. He could have helped her better, taken care of her.

"Don't tell my husband or daughters that there's something wrong with me. They depend on me. It'll be our little secret."

Should he tell her they knew? "Don't you think they might already know?"

"Do you think so?"

"Ja." He motioned toward the house. "Let me walk you to the house."

"All right. I still don't know why I came out here."

"To make my day." Seeing her had made him happy.

"You are a sweet one." She hooked her arm in his.

Halfway across the yard, Teresa stopped and pointed. "See those trees that edge our property?"

He nodded. A line of windbreak vegetation stood to the north.

"I want my *dawdy haus* right next to the highbush cranberry bushes."

A nice spot. "Why are you telling me?"

"So you know where to build it when the time comes."

She must be confused again.

"You want *me* to build your *dawdy haus*?"

"Of course. Who else?"

He didn't know what to say. Should he tell her he couldn't build it for her? Or hope this conversation was one she'd forget? If Deborah didn't stay, then he would leave, as well.

He cared deeply for this family.

And for a certain young woman.

Hannah came out of the house. *"Mutter?"*

"Over here." Amos guided Teresa toward her daughter. "Let's get you back inside."

Hannah rushed over. *"Mutter.* Don't go outside without telling anyone." She turned to Amos. *"Danki.* We thought you'd gone back home."

Not home, but she didn't need to know that. "I came back to talk to your *vater.* It's urgent."

"He's in the barn."

"Danki." As Amos crossed to the barn, he looked around the yard and at the newly sowed fields. He stared at the patch where Teresa Miller wanted her *dawdy haus.* He missed this place and its people—one most of all—even though he'd been gone for only one night.

Deborah's father pitched hay from the loft Amos had built. "Bartholomew."

Hay showered down, and he rested the pitchfork on the loft floor. "Amos. I thought you went back home."

Amos didn't want to take the time to explain just where he'd been. "We need to hurry. Deborah's leaving. We need to stop her."

"Ne. She's not."

"*Ja*. She is. There's… It's hard to explain, but if we both go, maybe we can talk her out of this foolishness."

Kittens scampered from the room Amos had occupied at the sound of his voice, meowing.

Bartholomew chuckled. "Someone was missed." He climbed down the ladder and gripped Amos's shoulders. "I know about the modeling. She was going to leave, but she's come to her senses."

"She has?" Amos gritted his teeth as two kittens climbed up his trouser legs, one in the front and one in the back. He plucked off the one in front. The other made it up on his shoulder. "She's staying?"

"*Ja*. She's staying."

Relief swept through Amos.

The older man stared up at the hayloft. "You did *gut* work. I won't be getting injured again." He waved an arm to include the surroundings. "It's back to me doing all the work around here. I appreciate all your hard work. You've done an excellent job with everything. I don't know how we would have managed without you."

"*Danki*." Teresa's words came back to him. What had she said? *He needs another man here.* That was the answer teasing him as he walked. "I'd like to stay on and continue to help you."

"What about going back to your family's farm? I'm sure they've missed you."

"The farm will go to my brothers. I believe this is where I'm supposed to be." This was where *Gott* had been preparing him for.

"Then you're welcome to stay. I'm not about to turn away help."

That pleased Amos. "But first, I have a confession."

"Bishop Bontrager is the one to hear confessions."

Telling Bartholomew Miller might not be necessary,

but Amos *needed* to do it if his plans were going to work out. "I have wronged you and need to ask your forgiveness."

"I can't think of anything you've done wrong. Whatever you think you've done, I forgive you."

That was nice, but Amos hadn't told him yet. "The whole time I was working here, I plotted to leave our community."

Bartholomew's eyebrows pulled down. "Leave the community?"

"I've changed my mind. I thought *Gott* was calling me away. I'd been hurt by…people. I figured if I was going to have to work in the *Englisher* world, I might as well live there, too."

"And?"

"I know I belong here." And not just in the community, but here on this farm. "Do you forgive me?"

Bartholomew rubbed his hand across his mouth. "It seems my farm has been harboring all kinds of secrets. *Ja.* I forgive you."

"Danki." Now for the hard part. Amos cleared his throat.

"Speak, boy. You obviously have something else to say. More secrets?"

Amos shook his head. "I would like…your permission to court—"

"Ja." A smile broke on the older man's face. "You have it."

Amos stood mute with his mouth hanging open, then found his voice. "But I haven't said which daughter."

"Deborah, of course."

How had he known? "Why not Miriam or Joanna?"

"Because you're not in love with either of them. You weren't thinking of asking for Miriam or Joanna, were you? Because that would have to be a different answer altogether."

"You would've said *ne*?"

"Of course."

"Why?"

"Because you're not in love with either of them. But you are with Deborah."

"Well, I wouldn't say I *love* her. Not yet. But I believe I'm on my way. And that's why I want to court her."

Bartholomew shook his head. "Young people can't see what's right in front of them, or know their own hearts."

Amos didn't know what the older man meant.

Bartholomew clasped Amos on the shoulder. "Trust me. This strange cacophony of emotions churning inside you that you're trying to sort out—that's love, boy."

Amos did have a myriad of emotions when it came to Deborah. But did they equal love? He didn't know.

But he aimed to find out.

Deborah stood on the shore of the pond with a heavy heart, watching the ducks and ducklings paddle around in the water.

Gott had wrestled with her most of the night. *Vater's* prayers had made her thrash about instead of sleeping, until she'd made the decision to stay. The right decision. She knew that in her soul. Though she hadn't gotten very much sleep, she felt surprisingly *gut*. Lighter.

She'd called Hudson early this morning to tell him to leave without her. He'd hung up on her.

Gott wanted her to stay with her family, which had been a great relief to her. What they were going to do about the medical bills, none of them knew, but if they could bring in a *gut* crop this year, they might scrape by. Thanks to Amos plowing and planting their crops for them, they had a chance to keep the farm, but it wouldn't be easy.

Oh, Amos. Why did he have to leave? She might never see him again. Her nose stuffed up with unshed tears, and she swallowed the lump in her throat. Was there anything she could say to convince him to return?

As though her thoughts caused him to appear, Amos approached. "*Hallo*, Deborah."

Was he really here? "Amos?"

"*Ja.* It's me."

His smile melted her heart, and she wanted to run to him but didn't. "What are you doing here? I thought you left."

"That's funny. I was going to say the same to you. I came to talk you out of leaving."

"I'm not leaving."

"Me either."

"But you were in town yesterday. I thought you'd already left. My *vater* said so."

"I had, but I couldn't sleep."

Just like Deborah. *Vater* must have been praying for him, too.

"I realized I didn't want to leave. I have been hurt a few times by girls I thought I wanted to marry. I decided that I couldn't trust any Amish girls. That's why I left."

And Deborah had fueled his mistrust by modeling and threatening to leave, as well.

He went on. "But *Gott* made me see that my trust was misplaced. I need to trust Him. I thought I wanted to leave, but I don't. I'm staying."

Dare she believe it. "You're staying? Really?"

"Really." He took her hand. "I've asked your *vater* permission to court you. He gave it."

Had she heard correctly? "You want to court *me*?"

"*Ja.*"

Part of her wanted to throw herself into his arms—something a *gut* Amish would *never* do. She'd definitely spent too much time in the *Englisher* world. Another part of her didn't believe his declaration could be true. Or at least, the declaration she'd imagined he'd said and dreamed he'd said.

"Are you going to give me your answer or continue to make me suffer?"

"I…I want to say *ja*, but I'm finding it hard to believe you would choose *me*. I haven't exactly been a model Amish."

"Who of us are perfect? None. And…"

"What?"

He chuckled. "I just realized your *vater* was right."

His laughter soothed her. "About what?"

"When I asked his permission to court you, he told me something. Something I didn't believe."

"What?"

"I don't know that I should say right now."

"Please." She wanted to know what her *vater* had said to make him smile like that. A smile that made her want to get lost in it.

"He told me that I was in love with you. I thought he'd gone daft."

Her heart soared. Loved? Dare she hope? "Go back. Say that again."

"I thought your *vater* was daft?"

"*Ne*. Before that."

His mouth pulled up on one side. "I asked perm—"

"After that."

Mischievousness played at the corners of his mouth.

He'd been teasing her.

He caressed the back of her hand with his thumb. "I love you, Deborah. I want to court you and marry you one day."

"I want that, too."

"Our own house and lots of children."

She sucked in a breath and pulled her hand away. "Oh, but I can't. I'm so sorry."

His smile slipped away. "If you're not ready, I'll wait."

The tears she'd held at bay before sprang to her eyes and blurred her vision. "It's not that." He was her dream come true. "I believe *Gott* wants me to remain here on my parents' farm the rest of my life to care for *Mutter*. So I can't marry."

"I want that, too. To stay on this farm. I've been trying to figure out where I belong. I felt *Gott* leading me away from my family's farm. I thought I was supposed to go out into the *Englisher* world. But that's not where He was leading me. He was preparing to send me here. Your *mutter* asked—*ne*—*told* me to build her a *dawdy haus* by the windbreak. I want to do that. Your *vater* has already given his permission for me to stay here. I want to live here and help take care of her. With you, of course."

Deborah had believed she needed to give up on the dream of marrying one day. Believed that was her penance for modeling. In spite of her poor choices in the past, *Gott* was giving her the desire of her heart.

"What do you say? Deborah Miller, will you marry me and be my wife?"

She did throw herself into his arms this time, and he caught her. "*Ja.* I want to be your wife." He lifted her off the ground and swung her around.

When he set her back down, he stared at her a moment with a huge grin, then he pressed his lips to hers.

A thrill tingled through her. "Well, now you'll have to marry me."

"Gladly." He kissed her again.

* * * * *

If you loved this story,
check out the previous book
in Mary Davis's miniseries
Prodigal Daughters

Courting Her Amish Heart

And if you like Amish stories,
be sure to pick up these books
by top author Jo Ann Brown
in her miniseries
Amish Spinster Club

The Amish Suitor
The Amish Christmas Cowboy

Available now from Love Inspired!

Find more great reads at www.LoveInspired.com

Dear Reader,

I hope you enjoyed the second book of the Prodigal Daughters miniseries, featuring Amish women with nontraditional hopes and dreams.

Before starting to write an Amish romance, I had to get to know who they were a little. Like a lot of people, I had preconceived notions of what the Amish were like. The more I researched the Amish, the more I fell in love with them. I learned things I never imagined and shattered the two-dimensional image I had of them and discovered a vibrant people.

I had so much fun coming up with these prodigal Amish women. As I said in the first book, I wanted to think of something an Amish person wouldn't do. Being a fashion model is high on that list. My next challenge was getting her away from her family farm all the time without her family noticing. I felt so bad for Deborah that her family didn't notice her regular absence, especially her *mutter*. So, I explored why they could be so callous toward her. If you've read this story, you know why, and if you haven't yet, I won't spoil it for you.

I loved getting to know Deborah and Amos and sharing their romance. Though Deborah may have thought she craved attention, she really just wanted to belong in her own family. Deborah's prodigality was selfish, but when her family needed her, she was willing to sacrifice everything for them.

Deborah is dear to my heart not only because my

heart ached for her misguided actions, but because I named her after my wonderful second oldest sister.

Until next time, happy reading!

Blessings,
Mary

COMING NEXT MONTH FROM
Love Inspired®

Available September 18, 2018

THE AMISH CHRISTMAS COWBOY
Amish Spinster Club • *by Jo Ann Brown*
Though Texan cowboy Toby Christner was raised Amish, he has no plans to settle down in the new community along Harmony Creek. But when he meets Amish nanny Sarah Kuhns, he can't help but wonder if a Plain life with her is exactly what he needs.

AN AMISH HOLIDAY WEDDING
Amish Country Courtships • Carrie Lighte
To bring in more revenue, Amish baker Faith Yoder needs to hire a delivery person to bring her treats to a nearby Christmas festival—and Hunter Schwartz is perfect for the job. They're both determined not to lose their hearts, but can they keep their relationship strictly professional?

THE RANCHER'S ANSWERED PRAYER
Three Brothers Ranch • by Arlene James
Tina Kemp's stepfather left her his house, but his nephew, Wyatt Smith, inherited the ranch—including the land the house stands upon. Neither is giving an inch. Can these adversaries possibly make a home together... without falling for each other?

CHRISTMAS WITH THE COWBOY
Big Heart Ranch • by Tina Radcliffe
At odds about the business they inherited, widowed single mother Emma Maxwell Norman and her late husband's brother, Zach Norman, must make a decision: sell, or run it together. Working side by side might just bring them the greatest Christmas gift of all—love.

WYOMING CHRISTMAS QUADRUPLETS
Wyoming Cowboys • by Jill Kemerer
Working as a temporary nanny for quadruplet babies, Ainsley Draper can't help but feel drawn to the infants' caring rancher uncle, Marshall Graham. But with her life in one town and his family obligations in another, can they ever find a way to be together?

THEIR FAMILY LEGACY
Mississippi Hearts • by Lorraine Beatty
When Annie Shepherd and her boys inherit her aunt's home, she never expects the man responsible for her family's tragedy to be living across the street. Can she keep punishing Jake Langford for his youthful mistake, or let love and forgiveness lead the way?

LICNM0918

Get 4 FREE REWARDS!

We'll send you 2 FREE Books plus 2 FREE Mystery Gifts.

Love Inspired® books feature contemporary inspirational romances with Christian characters facing the challenges of life and love.

FREE Value Over **$20**

SPECIAL EXCERPT FROM

Love Inspired®

*Though Texan cowboy Toby Christner was raised
Amish, he has no plans to settle down in the new
community along Harmony Creek. But when he meets
Amish nanny Sarah Kuhns, he can't help but wonder
if a Plain life with her is exactly what he needs.*

Read on for a sneak preview of
The Amish Christmas Cowboy *by Jo Ann Brown,
available in October 2018 from Love Inspired!*

Toby was sure something was bothering Sarah.

He thought through their conversation among her family's Christmas trees. She'd been distressed by how Summerhays and his wife paid too little attention to their *kinder*, but she'd been ready to speak her mind on that subject.

So what was bothering her?

You.

The voice in his head startled him. He'd heard it clearly and, for once, it wasn't warning him away from becoming too close to someone. Instead, it was telling him the reason why there might be a wall between him and Sarah.

Maybe it was for the best. Every day he lingered was another drawing him into the community. Each moment he spent with Sarah enticed him to look forward to the next time they could be together. In spite of his determination, his life was being linked to hers and her neighbors.

That would change once his coworker's trailer pulled up to take him back to Texas.

Sarah gestured toward the *kinder*. "They're hungry for love."

"You're worried they're going to be hurt when I go back to Texas."

"Ja."

He wanted to ask how she would feel when he left, but he'd hurt his ankle, not his head, so he didn't have an excuse to ask a stupid question.

"The *kinder* will be upset when you go, but won't it be better to give them nice memories of your times together to enjoy when they think about you after you've left?"

Nice memories of times together? Maybe that would be sufficient for the *kinder*, but he doubted it would be enough for him.

Don't miss
The Amish Christmas Cowboy *by Jo Ann Brown,*
available October 2018 wherever
Love Inspired® *books and ebooks are sold.*

www.LoveInspired.com

Looking for inspiration in tales
of hope, faith and heartfelt romance?

Check out **Love Inspired**® and
Love Inspired® **Suspense** books!

New books available every month!

Love Inspired®

Inspirational Romance to Warm Your Heart and Soul

Join our social communities to connect with other readers who share your love!

Sign up for the Love Inspired newsletter at **www.LoveInspired.com** to be the first to find out about upcoming titles, special promotions and exclusive content.

CONNECT WITH US AT:

Harlequin.com/Community

 Facebook.com/LoveInspiredBooks

Twitter.com/LoveInspiredBks

LISOCIAL2017